About the Author

By profession, Lance Thorburn is a consulting electrical engineer, but prior to this, he worked for the South African Broadcasting Corporation – SABC for a number of years. He is the pastor of a local church on the south coast of KwaZulu Natal. He has written two other novels – *Freedom's Price Tag* and *Just for Fun – Five Plus One* and has co-written a technical book called *South African Earthing Principles*. As a major in the SA Defence Force, he was editor of the monthly newsletter for The Gunners' Association – *Ubique*.

"I Cried for You, South Africa"

Lance Thorburn

"I Cried for You, South Africa"

Olympia Publishers
London

www.olympiapublishers.com
OLYMPIA PAPERBACK EDITION

Copyright © Lance Thorburn 2024

The right of Lance Thorburn to be identified as author of
this work has been asserted in accordance with sections 77 and 78 of
the Copyright, Designs and Patents Act 1988.

All Rights Reserved

No reproduction, copy or transmission of this publication
may be made without written permission.
No paragraph of this publication may be reproduced,
copied or transmitted save with the written permission of the publisher,
or in accordance with the provisions
of the Copyright Act 1956 (as amended).

Any person who commits any unauthorised act in relation to
this publication may be liable to criminal
prosecution and civil claims for damage.

A CIP catalogue record for this title is
available from the British Library.

ISBN: 978-1-80439-898-2

This is a work of fiction.
Names, characters, places and incidents originate from the writer's
imagination. Any resemblance to actual persons, living or dead, is
purely coincidental.

First Published in 2024

Olympia Publishers
Tallis House
2 Tallis Street
London
EC4Y 0AB

Printed in Great Britain

Dedication

This novel is dedicated to my wife, Jean. Without her love and dedication, this novel would not have been possible.

Foreword

Six people out of every seven worldwide believe in a higher being. Many scholars have devoted their complete lives to studying, and recording, one of the great religions of the human race. Some have come close to an understanding; some have paid the ultimate price for what they believe; and some have even stood up boldly, and dared to tell anyone who would listen, about their particular version of the truth.

It is fairly safe to say that each of us reserves our own thoughts when we are faced with the truth as told by learned men, and women, but we all deeply want to be on the side of this higher being.

Each of the world's religions, for the most part, promotes peace and goodwill amongst men, women and children, and yet governments pass laws that place people against people. Not only countries against countries but people within their own countries, against one another. What has the world learnt over all the millennia? One shudders at the thought, yet each day we awaken and secretly hope, and even pray, for a better day for ourselves and our children.

This story that you are about to read tells of a government policy that goes against every conceivable good that the world's great religions even contemplate. It is with sadness that I tell you what is happening in my own country, the place of my birth, South Africa. It brings me to my knees, as I cry for you, my dear land, South Africa.

Two forms of science, namely pharmaceutical and nuclear physics, talk of the 'half-life'. The term is foreign to most, and not normally used in everyday conversation. If any one of us, outside of these industries, spoke of a half-life, our listener would truly think we were trying to pull their leg or any other such misbelief.

The theory of the 'half-life' goes like this: Say you take a tablet for a simple dose of flu – that tablet will have what is called a 'half-life'. You can Google any tablet criteria, and one of the specifications is its half-life. Back then to our flu tablet! Let us say that it has a half-life of six hours, this means that it will reach its peak of efficiency six hours after you have swallowed it. But that is only half the story. As the theory goes, you will have to read the complete book before the second half becomes apparent.

Let us pause that explanation and continue it on the last page of the book.

The newly formed Nationalist government of 1948 called their particular form of government, 'separate development'. The world media soon found that the Afrikaans word for separate development was 'apartheid'. In its purest form, it was to govern people separately, according to their race. On the surface, many people agreed that it was not such a bad idea, as South Africa had such a diverse population. Each group would get its fair share according to its own traditions and customs.

But that didn't happen, and the architects of *apartheid* soon entrenched White minority rule and discrimination against non-White groups. These groups included Black people, who made up roughly 80% of the population; coloured 8.8% and Indians/Asians 2.5%. To understand why the *apartheid* system gained a foothold in South African society, we need to take a journey back in time to the year 1880, 20 December 1880 to be precise.

This was the start of what was known as the First Boer[1] War. It only lasted three months, ending on 23 March 1881. The Boer states of the Transvaal and the Vrystaat[2] were defeated by British colonial forces. All this First Boer War did was to set up the circumstances for a much more violent and prolonged war, the Second Boer War, from 11 October 1898 to 31 May 1902.

Again, the independent Boer states – the Transvaal and the Free State – took up arms against the British colonial forces based in Natal and the Cape. Both sides, Boers and British, took huge losses, estimated to include 28,000 British troops and 26,000 civilian deaths, of which 4000 were actual Boer soldiers.

It was a difficult war to fight from both sides' points of view. The Boers generally fought in small bands, much like what we would call guerrilla warfare today – strike and move, disrupt communications and mingle with the local population, typically very hard to engage.

On the other hand, the British Imperial troops certainly outnumbered the Boers, almost seven to one, and the methods of engagement were awkward, as their formations of infantry and cavalry, fought in blocks or lines, were useless and ill-advised in the drifts and hillsides of the Transvaal landscape. These British troops were easy pickings for the swift, small bands of Boer fighters, who could get in and out of a conflict with relative ease.

As the Boers started to feel the weight of the war, and the relentless number of British soldiers, coming wave after wave, they started a scorched-earth or burnt-earth policy. Everywhere

---

[1] Afrikaans word for farmer.
[2] Afrikaans word for Free State.

the Boers went, they set fire to the crops, the landscape, the houses, homesteads and even whole towns. This policy stretched from Bloemfontein in the south to Pretoria in the north. The unfortunate result of this was that the Boers' families suffered. The Boers took away the very resources that they, and their families, needed to survive.

Lord Roberts, the Commander of the British Imperial Forces, had no option but to round up huge numbers of Boer women and children and place them in camps, mainly to feed these unfortunate people. The Boers, however, didn't see it that way, and history records that these camps became known as concentration camps, a term that is still used today. These camps were ill-equipped, and thousands upon thousands of Boer women and children died, whilst in custody. This fact is probably one of the main contributing factors to the Boers' desperate desire, no, the need to take back or retain political power and self-determination for themselves. A little-known fact is that the British Colonial Forces set up sixty-six Black concentration camps. The apparent justification for this was to stop the Boers from getting supplies from the Black people.

By sheer weight of British numbers, a land that could not support a Boer fighting force, and the deaths of thousands in concentration camps, brought the Second Boer War to a halt, with the signing of The Treaty of Vereeniging on 31 May 1902. Yes, the British Empire had grown, but the damage was done. This war would remain fixed in the minds of the Boers, and would one day be avenged!

The years between 1902 and the next significant year, i.e. 1910, saw a consolidation of the Cape Colony, The Natal Colony (firmly under British rule), The Orange River Colony (Vrystaat) and the Transvaal, being spoils of the Second Boer

War, and to a lesser degree, South West Africa.[3] These colonies were consolidated into what was known as the Union of South Africa on 31 May 1910. This was passed into law by the British granting domination to the White minority, over the native Africans, Indians/Asians, and the so-called coloured people.

South Africa became a dominion of the British Empire – a new and hateful word had been born! General Louis Botha became the first Prime Minister, and General Jan Smuts was his deputy.

---

[3] Present-day Namibia.

Chapter 1

I got up from my knees, on which I had been praying in that remote little church that lay in the depths of the most beautiful garden.

The light of the morning sun was just bursting onto the windows that framed the east façade of the church structure. Here and there, the sunlight caught a shard of colourful glass, that formed an intricate part of the stained-glass window.

I had prayed to God, that this year would be different, that this start of the twentieth century would, at last, bring peace. I had just prayed that the Almighty, in all His greatness and wisdom, would set our country free. That we would be like no other, and that through the grace and wisdom of God, He would set people and families free to walk a path of harmony and peace with one another in a country so rich and yet so diverse.

"After all," I said to the Almighty, "there is certainly enough for us all to share."

It was 1900, the turn of a century, and a time that South Africa would prefer to forget. Excepting for three mothers, it would be a year the country wouldn't forget in a hurry!

The three mothers, and their extended families, had been preparing for this time, which would be a milestone in their lives. On 12 March 1900, the Van Wyk family welcomed a baby boy into the world. They had taken months pondering over a name for this baby. They needn't have worried because in

Boer family tradition, the eldest son was always given the name of his father, and his second name was that of his grandfather. So, this baby boy was baptised Sarel Jacobus Van Wyk in the Nederlandse Reformeerde Kerk[4] in Van Stadensrus – very near the Lesotho border.

A few weeks later, on 15 April 1900, and about 350 kilometres away from where Sarel was born, another baby boy came into the world. He was Fundile Khumalo, born in Kwagana in the Eastern Cape, not far from King Williamstown. In true Xhosa fashion, the family surname came from the clan or tribe into which the child was born. The Khumalo parents noticed that their new son was very clever, even at just a few days old, so they named him Fundile, which means 'smart' or 'educated' in isiXhosa.

During the much colder month of June, to be precise, on 16 June 1900, Michael John Porter-Smith was born in Johannesburg, to Mr and Mrs Robert Porter-Smith. This new baby boy was ceremoniously Christened in the Methodist Church, in the heart of Johannesburg. It was a splendid affair and the who's who of Johannesburg were invited to the occasion.

And so, the basis of our story begins with these three baby boys, who were born into contrasting families, in three different colonies, and into diverse cultures. The only thing they had in common was that they were all born in the year 1900!

---

[4] Afrikaans name for Netherlands Reformed Church.

Chapter 2

And then, as I prayed, a rather strange thing began to niggle its way into my subconscious thoughts. It was as if God was telling me to think about the different folk that made up the fabric of the society in which I lived.

"But, Dear Lord," I said, "there are just so many! Each group with its own needs and aspirations – each with its own agenda. How will I give fair time to each group?" I bumbled on, "Lord, there are farmers and industrialists, buyers and sellers; there are philanthropists, leaders and followers; there are rich and poor, young and old, the bold and the timid."

"Yes," said the Lord, "I know! I created each one of them. All I want you to do is choose any three families and set them apart, and be sure to pray for them each day and night. Don't worry about the rest, they are safe in My hands. You just pray for the three families that you choose."

As quickly as that instruction had come into my subconscious, it was gone!

And so, I started to pray, but this time, I had very clear instructions. Choose three families, and pray for them!

As my little church was originally built by missionaries, some fifty years ago, on a beautiful farm, it was easy to imagine and pray for a family who were farmers by choice.

"That was easy!" I said to the Lord. "I will make my first family a group of farmers!"

And so, I prayed, "Dear Lord, I bring to You... let's call them the Van Wyk family!"

As Sarel was the first of the three babies born, it is probably right, and fitting, to start with the older brother Piet, and tell of his circumstances first. But we are not.

"Kom binne!"[5] Sarel's mother called from the kitchen door. Sarel, and his slightly older brother, Piet, had been playing outside the farmhouse, with an old wagon wheel. Clouds were coming up, and vicious streaks of lightning were already flashing on the gentle slopes of the land.

Their mother was worried and hurried her two sons into the house. Their father was still out in the mielie[6] fields, but he would soon be on his way back to the house. Once in the homestead, Sarel and Piet had gone to their room to continue with the fantasy game they had been playing. Soon, Mrs Van Wyk heard the kitchen door opening, and in walked her husband, Koos. He was a giant of a man, and with his hat on, he stood well over six feet (two metres) tall.

Koos had been a Veldt Kornet[7] in the local Boer Commando, in the Vrystaat during the terrible First Boer War of 1880, but had luckily escaped with his parents soon after, and had settled nearer the Lesotho border. In those days, land was easily obtainable, and Koos' father was given land by the local Landdrost[8] under the terms of occupying as much land as you could circumnavigate in one day, on horseback. The result was that the farm they now occupied had a reasonably well-supplied small river running through its length. It was on the banks of

---

[5] Afrikaans phrase for 'Come inside'.
[6] Afrikaans word for 'maize/corn'.
[7] Afrikaans word for 'second lieutenant'.
[8] Afrikaans word for 'magistrate'.

this river that the family home had been built by Sarel's grandparents.

The lightning was followed by some good soaking rain, and just two hours later, the sun was shining again. "Dit was 'n lekker storm,"[9] said Koos, and continued, "just in time for the mielies and sonneblom[10] seeds to grow." Koos wasn't sure whether anyone had heard him.

However, eventually came, "Ja my lief!"[11] from the direction of the kitchen. "Kom eet nou."[12] Those words "*Kom eet nou*" reminded him of the time he and his friend had been to a farmers' meeting in the town about two years before. Word was out that the Union of South Africa was calling on men to fight in a new Anglo–German war.

"Nee![13] Not on your life am I going to help those bloody 'sout-piele'[14] fight a war!" The speaker at the meeting had even said that Black South Africans were going to fight alongside Whites. That was more than Koos could bear, so even when the braai[15] was ready and the chef had said, "Kom eet nou", he had got onto his horse and ridden home.

Petronella, Koos' wife, came through to the dining room with a hearty lunch of grilled meat and potatoes, which she carried on a tray, for Koos, Piet and Sarel. She put the food on

---

[9] Afrikaans for 'that was a nice storm'.

[10] Afrikaans word for 'sunflower'.

[11] Afrikaans for 'yes, my dear'.

[12] Afrikaans for 'come and eat'.

[13] Afrikaans word for 'no'.

[14] A very derogatory term in Afrikaans for the English-speaking South Africans, describing how they had one foot in South Africa, and the other in Britain, leaving their penises to hang in the salt water of the Mediterranean Sea.

[15] Afrikaans word for 'barbeque'.

the table, and called to the boys, "Kos is op die tafel."[16]

Both boys were growing and had good appetites, and were always hungry! They came running without a second invitation. The family gave thanks to the Almighty, for the food, which they did at the start of every meal, and then they began to eat in silence. It wasn't the place for children to speak without being spoken to. After all, Koos was the father, and Petronella and the boys had to respect the father's wishes, and family protocol at all times.

But on this occasion, the conversation moved to the subject of education. Piet being the older of the two boys was going to be eight years old in two months, and Sarel would turn six early the following year. The last time that Koos had ridden into town, he had heard that Tannie[17] Esterhuizen was going to start a plaasskool[18] on the outskirts of town. She had originally qualified as a teacher in Pretoria, in the old Boer Republic, and came highly recommended. The other farmers in the area agreed that this was a good idea, as many of them had children old enough for formal education. They had got together and built a mud brick building with a thatched roof for this purpose.

So, at lunch that day, Koos told his family of his plan. At the beginning of the next year, in three months' time, Piet and Sarel would begin school to learn to read and write, as Koos explained to them. Koos also explained to them all that Piet, as the eldest son, would inherit the farm one day. This saddened Petronella but she knew that this was the norm and there was little, or nothing, she could do about it.

"For that matter, it is important for Sarel to get an

---

[16] Afrikaans for 'food is on the table'.
[17] Afrikaans word for 'Aunty' or 'Miss'.
[18] Afrikaans word for farm school.

education, as he will have to go out and find work, someday soon!"

Petronella just smiled, but her heart was breaking for Sarel – everything was stacked in Piet's favour!

Chapter 3

By now, my prayer was developing, and even though my knees were hurting as I prayed, I asked God to lead me to the next group of people whom I should pray for.

My mind led me again to think about this little missionary church, in which I prayed.

What were the missionary preachers like? What did they teach about during the services held here on a Sunday? Did they preach on love and understanding, or were they more solemn, declaring only the do's and don'ts of life? What had indeed been said inside these hallowed walls? This led me to realise that this place of worship had also been used during the week as a school for the local children.

What was life like? What were the teachers like? How many children came each day? Their studies would have been so different from what I knew today! But the basics, I agreed with myself, would have been the same. Arithmetic and reading and writing came immediately to mind. The three 'R's' I reminded myself – 'Rithmetic, Reading and 'Riting as someone once joked.

I thought of boys and girls walking from their rural villages to school each day, here in the mission church / school where I was now on my knees praying.

"That's it, Lord!" I exclaimed. "Thank You! I will pray for someone whom I will call Fundile. Lord, let's say his family are called the Khumalo family!"

And so, I agreed. This will be the second group of people that I will pray for. I rubbed my poor aching knees and continued to pray.

The month of April was quite mild in the hills of the Eastern Cape, so on 15 April, when Fundile Khumalo was born, there had been no need to provide extra blankets for the new baby and his mother.

The birth was uncomplicated, and the many ladies of the small community rallied around to assist with the delivery. They had done this a few times before, as Fundile's mother had produced four baby girls, one each year, and now with this new baby, they, at last, had a boy!

At midday on the day after the birth, the men of the village slaughtered a young bull, to give recognition to the ancestors for the fact that the new baby was a boy. As Fundile's mother breastfed him in the thatched homestead, she could hear the village men talking outside as they prepared the meat and drank the local brew. The birth of this baby boy was truly a great occasion in the village of Kwagana.

Family life in the Khumalo household was simple. They lived in a kraal,[19] and the Khumalos had four circular mud huts surrounded by a fence, made of some old tree branches and some logs. This fence was to keep out stray animals and to keep their own livestock inside. The fence also demarcated the land that belonged to the Khumalos.

The land tenure was a complicated one to follow. As Mr Khumalo senior understood it, the land had been allocated to his father by the local chief. Of course, there were no documents, no points of demarcation, just an understanding, that this piece

---

[19] Afrikaans word for 'compound'.

of land belonged to the Khumalos and would do, as long as the family existed. The adjacent land of rolling hills and valleys, where the cattle grazed, belonged to the tribe and was a common area at the behest of the chief.

The summers and winters came and went. The winters sometimes brought a brushing of snow. The cattle and goats produced their offspring, and the older cattle were slaughtered when the time came, and the younger ones produced milk and existed as a sign of the Khumalo's wealth.

Many years before, Khumalo senior had managed to trade for some seeds, and at this stage, they were producing enough mielies, pumpkins and beans to fulfil their needs, and even had a little extra to sell, to buy clothes for themselves, and even a luxury like jam, from the general store. It was a hand-to-mouth existence, with everyone relying on each other, to pull their weight for the good of the collective.

It always caused deep sorrow in the heart of Fundile's father when he thought about the crops. It reminded him of his late brother, Dlamini Khumalo, who had served in the South African Army and was drowned at sea in 1916, off the coast of the Isle of Wight. Dlamini and six hundred and forty-six fellow Black South Africans drowned on the *SS Mendi* after being hit by the *SS Darro*. The family could never really understand why his body could not have been sent home for a traditional Xhosa burial.

On a certain sunny day, Thabile, Fundile's mother, took him on a visit to the local Roman Catholic Mission. The nuns at the mission station had been in the area for as long as Thabile could remember. She always enjoyed her trips to the mission and enjoyed the company of the European women, dressed in their long grey habits, tied in the middle with a belt, and of course, they wore veils on their heads, hiding any vestiture of hair. Thabile always eyed the beads that hung around their necks with a wooden cross, firmly attached to the last bead with a piece of string. These nuns were from Scotland and spoke with a very strange accent. Thabile was delighted that they could speak a little of her own language, and always laughed at the way they pronounced the words. These Scottish nuns had taught Thabile to say, "Top of the morning to you!" She had practised and practised, and today she was quite proficient in her greeting of the nuns when she arrived at the mission.

The nuns were very excited to meet Fundile. They, of course, had met his sisters, who had been brought to the nuns for help when they had not been well. This meeting with the boy of the household was special, and the nuns organised some tea and biscuits in his honour. This meeting was not only to show off her six-year-old son, but it was also to ask the nuns to teach him to read and write. Thabile knew that they had a small school in the back of the chapel because she had seen it before, and she wasn't sure how to speak about this as her language was a barrier to getting her request across.

She decided to give it a go, but she stumbled over the words and began to cry. Fundile wasn't helping matters either, as he was running around, laughing and shouting as young boys do. Seeing her distress, one of the senior nuns instructed a younger nun to take Fundile for a walk in the garden.

Sister Jean put her arms around Thabile and the conversation started again. This time, they understood what she was asking. "Of course," said the kindly Sister Jean. "He can come to school after Christmas." This made Thabile cry even more. She said thank you by clapping her hands, called for Fundile and left the mission station.

How was she going to tell her husband? In the Xhosa tradition, only the fathers made important decisions like this. Who would look after the cattle, sheep and goats as they grazed on the nearby hills?

Chapter 4

My prayer concentration was broken for a minute or so, when a little, brightly coloured bird actually knocked on the window pane not far from where I was praying.

'Tap! Tap!' was the sound of its beak on the glass pane. I watched in awe as it then preened itself, pecked at the window again as if to greet me, and flew off – glad to be free in such a beautiful place.

I reprimanded myself for breaking my concentration and closed my eyes once more. I had thought of a farmer and also a family living near this mission station. Who could be my third group? I pondered this question, and it took longer than I had thought. Just then, like a steam train coming along the tracks at full speed, the answer came to me. The opposite end of the scale, I said to myself. The opposite end of the scale! But who is that? What does 'the opposite end of the scale' mean? Please help me, Lord, I prayed.

By now my knees were really hurting. Lots of people went through my mind – the rich, the ultra-poor, the sick, the sad and the lonely. And then it came to me! What about an ordinary suburban family? Those whom you would see at the shops, or out for a Sunday drive. An ordinary family of moderate means, who make their living in a business in one of the cities.

So, I settled on the family that I would call the Porter-Smiths. Maybe a bit presumptuous of me, but Porter-Smith fitted the profile! So, again I prayed.

June was probably the coldest month in Johannesburg. The town had grown rapidly since the discovery of gold in 1886 by the prospector, George Harrison.

From its dusty camp town status run by a health committee and only gaining municipal status in 1897, Johannesburg had become, over the last thirteen years, a typical town on the gold reef, bustling with foreigners from all over the world, trying to prospect and make a fortune.

Michael John's parents, the Porter-Smiths, had originally come from Kimberley, which was a diamond area, where they had sought their fortune in diamonds. But in 1890, they moved to Johannesburg in favour of the more lucrative gold find. Michael John would one day tell his grandchildren that his parents had owned the first brick house in Johannesburg.

His parents made some good money in the early days of Johannesburg, and would probably have been called middle class. Being English-speaking in 1900 meant that you were clearly not part of the Boer Republic, but were actually in favour of British rule. Laws had been passed in London, very far away, granting domination to the White minority, over the native Africans, Asians and coloured people. Johannesburg, with the rest of South Africa, would become a dominion of the British Empire, and eventually, Louis Botha would become the first Prime Minister, with Jan Smuts as his deputy.

Nationalism was rife amongst the population, and in 1912, Michael John's father had heard that the natives had formed what was called the African National Congress. This raised a few eyebrows! Not many people cared. After all, everyone in Johannesburg was too busy thinking about gold and all the luxuries that this would ultimately bring. Those who were politically minded got together, and in 1914 the National Party was formed. This was the start of South African nationalism.

27

When Michael John was born in 1900, his father was already starting to climb the ladder of success. Not as fast as some of the other gold barons, but comfortably enough. So much so that the family soon became foundation members of the newly formed Methodist Church on Jeppe Street.

As the congregation grew, it became apparent that some form of musical instrument would be needed, and they borrowed a well-worn piano that had belonged to the saloon.

"No!" said Mr Porter-Smith. "I will donate a pipe organ to the church. It is far more proper." With that, a beautiful peddle pipe organ, complete with candelabra, was ordered from Cape Town, some one thousand miles away, and it was shipped all the way by ox wagon. It took over three months, but it eventually arrived, to the delight of the congregation, in Johannesburg.

In 1914, when World War I broke out between England and Germany, the British government realised that they had a German colony right on the western border of the newly formed Union of South Africa. Hastily, an army was raised amongst the population of the Union, which resulted in 146,000 Whites and 83,000 Blacks signing up. They were dispatched under the title of the South African Union Defence Force to German South West Africa and later, on to Delville Wood in France. Michael John's Uncle Harry volunteered, and fought with distinction, thankfully coming home a decorated hero.

Michael John grew up like hundreds of other boys, born to gold-prospecting families. The dust roads between the houses, with the ever-growing buildings, became their playground. They witnessed oxen pulling heavily laden wagons, spurred on by drivers with whips, cracking every so often to encourage them to pull a little harder. Later came the horse-drawn 'surreys' with pretty ladies sitting in the seats, with their long skirts and hats. The boys would wave as they went by, and sometimes a naughty boy would throw a stone, and the lead horse would shy and start galloping, causing the driver to shout, "Steady on!"

Pure delight came on a day when they saw a two-wheeled bicycle come past. Each boy would dream of the day when they would each have one to ride down to the river and into the veld.[20] This was surely their dream.

The boys in Michael's immediate group were now between eight and ten years of age, and their days were carefree. In the last six years after becoming the Union of South Africa in 1910, the Union began building and establishing schools for White children to attend. So it was that Michael John, now ten years old, was enrolled at the Jeppe Boys and Girls School in 1910, in the leafy suburb of Jeppe Town. Before attending school, Michael John was home-schooled by his mother. The Porter-Smiths were so impressed with the school that they purchased a property in Jeppestown, and proceeded to build a new brick house with a shiny corrugated iron roof.

At about the same time, Michael's mother and father increased the family, by giving him three sisters. Times were reasonably good for the family, and the father set himself up as a highly successful builder. There was a huge need for housing and buildings in the ever-growing Johannesburg and surrounding areas, and Mr Porter-Smith saw an opportunity and seized it with both hands.

School days were excellent for Michael John and his various sisters. They were indeed privileged! Their manners were excellent, and the teachers were kind, even though Michael John thought they were strict.

---

[20] Afrikaans word for 'meadow' or 'grasslands'.

Chapter 5

By now, my knees were extremely sore, and I had no option but to get up and sit on one of the beautifully crafted pews in the church. I apologised to the Lord, but my knees were truly aching now!

Sitting in the pew, looking at the stain-glass window before me, I realised just how fortunate I was, and how the years had been kind to me.

I had a good education and a comfortable set of work conditions. When feeling hungry, I simply had to open the cupboard door, and there was a choice of all sorts to eat. Seldom had I given thought to the farmer who had toiled on the land to provide the corn and grain that would make my morning cereal. Yes, I always said grace before a meal, but often gave little thought to the farmer who had produced it!

Soon, I thought about the characters in the Van Staden family – Koos, Sarel and Piet on the farm. They were very real people, and they were given the opportunity of producing food for the population.

How dependent they were on the soil and God providing rain at exactly the right time during the growing seasons! It wasn't easy being a farmer these days, and I was sure that it was doubly difficult years ago!

As I sat in the pews, I considered what references the Word of God supplied on the subject of the first and second born of the sons in a family.

I thought of Cain, the first son of Adam, and Abel the second son, and how the Lord had accepted Abel's offering, but not that of Cain. One up for the second-born!

I thought of Ishmael, Abraham's first son, and Isaac his second son. Two – nil for the second son, I noted. Esau and Jacob – another win for the second son! Three – nil depending on which faith you follow.

My mind turned back to Piet and Sarel of Van Stadensrus. Would Piet or Sarel win this narrative?

Sarel finished school, at the Van Stadensrus Primere en Sekondere Skool[21] at the age of fifteen. He passed out with a standard eight certificate. His brother, Piet, had done the same two years earlier. Neither of the boys was very good academically. It didn't matter that much for Piet, because he would inherit the family farm, Jakkalsfontein,[22] and so employment wasn't an issue. The farm consisted of a homestead, outbuildings and livestock, and Piet would take over once his father retired. But for Sarel, leaving school meant an end to the little security he did have.

There were few or no job opportunities in the town. Koos took Sarel to town one day on the insistence of his wife Petronella to see if the local farmers cooperative had any work but at this time, the farming community was still getting over the employment woes of the 1922 strike, four years earlier.

The strike had started on 28 December 1921 but by the time the news arrived in Van Stadensrus, eight hundred kilometres away, it was already 1922. Koos had gone to town that morning to purchase provisions from the Co-op. There

---

[21] Afrikaans for 'Primary and Secondary School'.
[22] Afrikaans for Jackals Fountain.

were other farmers there at the time, and Oom[23] Ben Van Der Raahd was reading to them all from the Eastern Free State Dispatch that was published in a town called Bloemfontein. This newspaper took four days, from the date of printing, to reach Van Stadensrus.

But it was news and all those gathered were listening while Oom Ben read to them from the paper. From the report in the Dispatch, the White miners, particularly in the areas of Brakpan and Benoni,[24] had gone on strike, and this had led to associated mining industries joining in the industrial action. Oom Ben stopped to light his pipe. "Gaan aan,[25] Oom Ben!" complained one of the farmers in the crowd.

Ben puffed on his pipe and then continued. The gold price had apparently dropped from 130 shillings to 95 shillings in the past week. This caused a stir among the farmers gathered. This would have a ripple effect on the price of mielies, in about three months!

"Stilte!"[26] said Ben, and read on. It appeared, according to the report, that the owners of the mines had decided to reduce the numbers of White miners, at their high salaries, and replace them with cheaper Black labour.

This last part of the report drew consternation from those gathered.

"Dis 'n skande!"[27] retorted Japie, who was standing next to Koos. "Hoe kan wit mense hul werk verloor, en swartes die

---

[23] Afrikaans for 'uncle'.

[24] Towns of the gold reef about thirty kilometres from Johannesburg.

[25] Afrikaans for 'go on'.

[26] Afrikaans for 'quiet'.

[27] Afrikaans for 'This is a scandal'.

geld kry?"[28] continued Japie. All those around him agreed that this was not right. Japie concluded, "Ons moet 'n plan maak, om hierdie swartes te segredeer.[29] Koos had gone home upset after the meeting in town, wondering how such a thing could happen. He would ask Oom Ben to read next week's newspaper to him.

The following Sunday, the Van Wyk family went to church, as was their culture. It took them about an hour on the horse-drawn cart, but going to church was the most important event of the week for the Van Wyk family and others. The Dominee[30] greeted them each by name, and when he got to Sarel, he asked, "Het jy werk gekry?"[31]

"Nee, *Dominee*," he replied.

Koos overheard the conversation and cut in, realising that the minister was in contact with so many people, as well as being a very learned man. So he asked if the minister could perhaps advise the family where Sarel could obtain work.

The minister answered immediately that they should go to Bloemfontein and speak to the clerk at the railway office, as they were looking for young men to train.

"Dankie,[32] *Dominee,*" said Koos, for the much-appreciated lead and advice. Koos hardly heard the sermon that morning as he thought about how he was going to travel the three hundred kilometres to Bloemfontein, at that time. After all, it was 'oostyd'[33] in the next few weeks, and travelling to Bloemfonein

---

[28] Afrikaans for 'How can White people lose their jobs and Blacks get the money?'

[29] Afrikaans for 'We must make a plan to segregate the Blacks'.

[30] Afrikaans for 'minister'.

[31] Afrikaans for 'Have you found a job?'

[32] Afrikaans for 'thank you'.

[33] Afrikaans for 'harvest time'.

and having to stay somewhere would take over a week, let alone the cost!

Koos was so deep in thought that Petronella had to nudge him to stand for the benediction. On the ride home, Koos consolidated his thoughts, and by the time they reached the homestead, he had made a plan. The only problem was where they would be able to stay in Bloemfontein while they spoke to the railway clerk.

Once they had seen to the horse being fed and watered, Petronella went to make tea. Koos took her aside and explained his plan to her. She expressed deep concern and again suggested that Koos split the farm between the two boys. "Nee, my vrou. Dis nie reg nie!"[34] She dared not argue further, as it was not the woman's place to doubt her husband's decision. Deep in her heart, though, she knew this would lead to failure.

When it came to helping Koos with his plan, Petronella suggested that Koos and Sarel should allow three days, at least, for travelling to Bloemfontein, and that they should add a few extra hours, so that they could rest the horses regularly. Koos agreed with this suggestion. She then suggested that they could find accommodation with Tannie Flo in Bloemfontein. She was, after all, Koos' direct cousin! Koos's face contorted at this suggestion, and the veins in his neck grew thicker. Petronella was worried that something was wrong with him.

"Wat is fout?"[35] she asked. She had inadvertently struck a nerve by raising a memory which Koos had vowed he would never allow surfacing again. Many years ago, long before Koos was born, his uncle, Oom Gert, had slept with a Black woman, and as a result, Flo had been born. Flo was a year or two older

---

[34] Afrikaans for 'No, my wife. That is not right'.
[35] Afrikaans for 'What is wrong?'

than Koos and no one in the immediate family had ever spoken of the disgrace of Flo being coloured. Piet and Sarel didn't even know of her existence.

"Waarvandaan kom al hierdie strond?"[36] was her husband's reply, once he had regained his composure. Only then did the secret come out that Petronella and Flo had been corresponding, on the sly! Koos again went bright red, and he stormed out of the house, for a walk in his mielie fields.

About five hours later, Petronella had prepared a roast with fresh vegetables for dinner, and this was sufficient to get Koos off the land, and back into the house once more. He had calmed down and Petronella thought it prudent not to mention Flo again for a while, even though she believed that Flo would offer Koos and Sarel the accommodation they would need for a few days while in Bloemfontein. After supper was over, and while the family were enjoying a nice cup of percolated coffee, Koos explained the plans for the trip.

*

Sarel was slightly over the age of twenty when he completed his apprenticeship on the South African Railways. He qualified as a fitter and turner, specialising in steam engine boilers. His salary was meagre, but he had been assured by the railways that he would receive a good pension when he turned sixty. He would be entitled to twenty-one days of paid leave a year. As a member of the railways, he and his family would be allowed to receive medical treatment at the provincial hospital for free. This was worth something, and Sarel was pleased with his

---

[36] Afrikaans for 'Where is all this nonsense coming from?'

general situation.

The next hurdle was to regularly check the notice board in the station concourse for vacant positions being posted. He didn't have to wait long, for two positions to be advertised for 'class one boiler makers'. One position was in Durban, and the other in Johannesburg, at the works in the Braamfontein depot.

He immediately went to see the recruitment officer and after much deliberation, he settled for the position in Johannesburg because there were probably more Afrikaans-speaking people there than in Durban, where Sarel believed there were mostly 'rooinekke'.[37]

The approval of his application took a full two weeks and, reluctantly after four years, Sarel said goodbye to Tannie Flo, and boarded a train bound for Johannesburg.

The next four years saw Sarel's career going from strength to strength. He was very good at his work, and soon he was assigned a Black man, Phineus, to carry his toolbox, if he had to work on a locomotive any walking distance away. Sarel never learnt to speak Phineus's language, even though they worked together every day. It amazed Sarel, though, that each day, his helper seemed to learn a new Afrikaans word and he soon understood what Sarel was saying.

When Sarel arrived in Johannesburg four years earlier, he quickly learnt that accommodation was expensive, especially on his salary, so he had asked around and was directed to the railway flats in Doornfontein. This accommodation was partially sponsored by the railways, so Sarel had decided that,

---

[37] Afrikaans for 'red necks' – a derogatory term for the English – the name coming from the British soldiers, who had fought in the First and Second Boer Wars, and whose uniform collars were red.

although the flats were very basic, it would suit him for the next while. After all, the flats were only two kilometres from the works in Braamfontein, and they were for Whites only.

The subsequent years brought mixed successes and failures for Sarel. Not long after moving into his apartment in Doornfontein, he got word from home that his father had passed away. His brother was now, of course, in charge of the farm. The letter had come from his mother, who had regularly kept in contact with him. The letter also said that Piet had married a girl called Rosa, from the adjoining farm, and that Rosa had suggested that Piet build a cottage on the farm for his mother as far enough away that the young people would not disturb her! Petronella laid out her heart in the letter, telling Sarel that it had broken her heart to move out of her house into the much smaller one-bedroom cottage. She had closed off by asking Sarel to come and visit her as soon as he could.

*

The Nationalist Party was in power under Prime Minister J B Hertzog. Sarel had voted for the party at the last election, purely because the party had voted to remove Black people from the common voter's roll. But now, in 1934, Hertzog had been talking to the old South African Party, to join the Nationalist Party, and form a common United Party. Sarel wasn't too sure about this, as he feared that the party would lose its Afrikaans flavour! Sarel chuckled when he remembered that the party had given women the vote a few years back!

One of these young women was a certain Magdelien Du Preez. She worked as a receptionist at the YWCA in Doornfontein, a building that Sarel passed every day on his way to work. The first time they had set eyes on one another, she was just walking up the steps of the building, to the main door. Sarel put his hand to his cap in a kind of salute but did not remove the cap as every good young man knew to do. The next time he saw her was a few days later when he found Magdelien fiddling in her handbag. Sarel was never sure whether the handbag had fallen by mistake, or on purpose as he passed, but he immediately went down and retrieved the bag and its contents that were strewn on the pavement. He gathered everything up, handed the bag back to Magdelien, doffed his cap and went on his way.

But the trick had worked, and the next time he passed her on the staircase going up to the YWCA, he found the courage to address her and to his delight, she replied in perfect Afrikaans. She was a little nervous at first, but as the days went by, their meetings became more confident, and they started speaking openly.

One Friday afternoon, Sarel was passing her place of work, when he found her standing on the stairs. He had a brown paper bag under his arm, wrapping a bottle of brandy, that he had bought at the bottle store on his way home. He stopped to chat with her and suddenly felt confident enough to ask her to go out with him.

"Madelien, sal jy more, saam met my dieretuin toe gaan?"[38] There! He had said it! She agreed, and they made arrangements to meet the next morning. Sarel went home and poured himself a dop brandewyn.[39] Tomorrow was going to be a good day!

The pair met the next morning and walked from

---

[38] Afrikaans for 'Will you go with me to the zoo tomorrow?'
[39] Afrikaans for 'tot of brandy'.

Doornfontein to the suburb of Saxonwold. The area, Saxonwold, had been given to the Health Committee of Johannesburg, as a gift in 1904, by the gold mining magnate, Herman Eksteen, for the sole purpose of a recreational area for the people of the city. A little later, the zoo was established and given to the Johannesburg Municipality, to maintain and care for. Multiple trees had been donated and planted, and by now, Saxonwold, and its zoo, was a worthwhile place to visit.

And so, the pair walked from Doornfontein, over the hill, and down into Saxonwold. Sarel paid the modest entrance fee, and they wandered through the lanes that housed the cages of the various animals. They laughed and chuckled at the antics of some of the animals, and at what each other said. Eventually, they sat on one of the benches, tired from all the walking. Magdelien opened her handbag, the same one Sarel had picked up the other day, and took out two cheese and tomato sandwiches, neatly wrapped in brown paper.

Sarel was truly impressed and told her that he would go to the kiosk and buy two bottles of lemonade. On his return, they enjoyed their food and drink, while they chatted away, covering all sorts of topics, until late in the afternoon. Sarel then insisted that they make their way home before it got too dark.

The climb back up the hill into Braamfontein was quite steep and tiring, and Sarel offered his hand to Magdalien, to help her. That had all happened two years ago, and now Sarel and Magdelien were married. He still worked at the railway depot in Braamfontein, and she was still at the YMCA as the senior receptionist, after getting a small promotion. They were still in the flats in Doornfontein but had now moved into a two-bedroom unit.

Chapter 6

As I pondered who would be given dominance in these pages, the older or the younger brother, my concentration was interrupted once again, this time by a cow lowing in the field some distance away! The sound was almost forlorn, and I rather hoped that another cow would have an answering call! But nothing came. Maybe it was just what cows do when they stand in a field!

Was this the same for me, or anyone else who would like to be included in this question?

Does my voice, my plea, my cry, just remain unanswered; does the sound of my call just vanish into the ether somewhere, never to be heard again?

Or, does it, in fact, get heard? Does God hear the call, and analyse if it is desperate, genuine or just a call? I would like to believe that our calls and our prayers are heard and that the Almighty acts on the urgent, and laughs with us when we just make a noise!

But it had to be more complex than this, I conceded, shifting my weight in the pew. Yet, there are rituals and there are solemn days when each of us pleads allegiance to our Maker and on those days, we make promises and commit ourselves to be upright and honest people.

We are thankful and pray for assistance. Surely, I thought, on days like these, our Maker, the Omnipresent, hears our call and as we take our first steps into adulthood and the unknown,

He indeed listens very carefully!

Watching the cattle with the other boys each day had taught Fundile many bush-crafting skills. Now that he was nearing his sixteenth birthday, his parents had discussed his Ulwaluko[40] with him. His father had explained that now he was older, he would have to learn the responsibilities of an adult, and that Ulwaluko was a special ritual, a cultural tradition, and a rite of passage to manhood.

His mother, Thabile, didn't add much to the conversation, as she was very confused. Fundile had been attending the Catholic Mission School each morning for several years but now his father was in the process of explaining initiation to him, the spiritual implications and that it was the basis of ancestral worship. It was not her place to speak at this time. After all, they had buried Fundile's umbilical cord the day after his birth, right next to the tree where they were now sitting!

Fundile nodded as his father spoke but, at the same time, he was truly excited and keen to undergo the experience. So, when the family went to sleep, Thabile whispered to her son, "Ulale Kamnandi."[41] Fundile was counting down the days to the ceremony when he would be an Abakhwetha.[42]

Soon the colder months approached and the young men in Fundile's village, and those of the surrounding villages, were assembled for the annual initiation ceremony – the Khweta.[43] This ceremony was an absolute must in any Xhosa boy's life. It is the passage from boyhood to manhood. The only personal

---

[40] IsiXhosa word for 'male initiation ritual'.
[41] IsiXhosa for 'Sleep well'.
[42] IsiXhosa word for 'initiate'.
[43] IsiXhosa for 'circumcision ceremony'.

belonging that Fundile was allowed to take with him was a blanket that his mother gave him.

All the boys gathered, made their way to the 'circumcision lodge', and immediately fell under the command of the lodge master. The events in the lodge were highly secretive, and no one may ever speak out later. Fundile had to put on a strange circumcision costume, and had to have his body painted with white sandstone, which he learnt later was to keep out the evil spirits, and then he covered himself with his blanket.

During the ceremony, Fundile also had to wear a skirt made out of reeds, and similarly, he had a cap made of reeds on his head, and he had to cover his face with the obligatory reed mask. Dressed in this paraphernalia, he joined his fellow initiates in a special dance, where the boys had to imitate a bull. They pawed the ground and tossed their heads as if they were raging bulls, snorting. The boys lost themselves in the dance, in a trance-like state, and drummed their heels into the ground, as they moved about!

Later, the circumcision was performed, and then the boys had to surrender their costumes and any other item they had used, including Fundile's mother's blanket. These things were thrown into the circumcision hut, which is then set alight. From there, the boys had to run to the river, and are ceremoniously thrashed, by the master, as they passed by. Fundile remembered each blow to his body, but he remembered how he ran, not being allowed to look back.

In the river, the last signs of boyhood were washed off! He entered the river as a boy and emerged as a man. At this time, each initiate was given a formal gift, a blanket, from their fathers. The boys were then smeared with red clay, which was not to be removed for three months. When it was eventually washed off, Fundile was regarded as a man of the tribe, and four years later, he would be able to marry.

Eighteen months passed and then one day, after Fundile had herded the cattle and goats safely into their holding area, he went to speak to his father. As was the custom, he went and sat beside the fire at his father's feet, while his mother prepared the evening meal. It was not his place to start a conversation, so he waited for his father to address him. He waited a good ten minutes before his father said, "Yebo, Fundile."[44]

Fundile had rehearsed what he would say many times, while he was out watching the herds, and now it was time to speak. "Utata, Umama,"[45] he began. He included his mother as he knew she would be listening from her cooking area. "Next year, I will be eighteen, and I was wondering if you would allow me to go and find work at eGoli..."[46] There was a pregnant silence, as he waited for the reaction.

Finally, his father cleared his throat, took out his clay pipe, and filled it with tobacco which he pressed down hard, then he took a burning coal from the fire and lit the pipe. Once he had drawn on it, the aroma filled the air and he cleared his throat again. "Nyana,[47] you have served our Usapo[48] well. We will be sad to see you go, but you are a man now, and it is time for you to leave." That is all he said, and Fundile understood every word. His mother kept on stirring the pot of Ipapa[49] and smiled.

The stage was set! Early the next morning, Fundile called his mother to help him. He had very few personal belongings,

---

[44] IsiXhosa for 'Yes, Fundile'.
[45] IsiXhosa for 'Father, Mother'.
[46] IsiZulu for 'place of gold' or 'gold mines'.
[47] IsiXhosa for 'son'.
[48] IsiXhosa for 'family'.
[49] IsiXhosa for 'porridge'.

but he did have two pairs of shoes – well, one pair was rubber sandals that he wore when he took the cattle out, and a pair of Sunday shoes, which his mother had bought from the nuns some years ago. His other possessions were two shirts and a pair of long pants, but that was not what he was looking for to pack.

He called out to his mother again, and when she finally came to him, he asked, "Umama, have you seen my Isatifiethi[50] from the mission school?"

"Be calm, my son. I have put it in a safe place."

"Enkosi,"[51] he said to his mother and hugged her. This certificate was Fundile's most treasured possession, apart from the wooden cross, that he wore around his neck on a piece of string. This certificate showed that he had passed standard two (fourth grade) with English and arithmetic. This was his 'Open Sesame' to the mining industry in Johannesburg.

The next Monday was a sad day for those staying behind in the Khumalo house but for Fundile, it was a great day of adventure. His mother prepared isidlo sasemini[52] for him to take with him. A few days prior, his father had sold one of the best goats, and he gave the proceeds to his son to buy a one-way train ticket to the gold fields, and the nuns had given him a small cardboard suitcase and a new flat cap, for his trip.

Fundile checked that he had his certificate in his pocket because he didn't trust putting it in the suitcase, which could easily be stolen in the third-class rail carriage. The farewell was sad! His mother and sisters cried, and his father asked the

---

[50] IsiXhosa for 'certificate'.
[51] IsiXhosa for 'Thank you'.
[52] IsiXhosa for 'lunch'.

ancestors to watch over him. The family had no idea when and if they would see him again. In these parts, news travelled very slowly.

The train trip was long and tiring, but as this was his first trip on a train and even the first time that he had travelled away from home, Fundile enjoyed watching the world go by, as the train made its way to his new life of adventure.

At last, the train puffed its way into Park Station, in Braamfontein, Johannesburg. Everyone climbed out, and everyone, except for Fundile, seemed to know where they were going. He walked out of the station and found himself on the corner of two streets – Rissik and Wolmarans streets. The names meant nothing to him, but it was getting late, and he didn't want to have to sleep on the street.

He tried to engage other Black folks in conversation, but most of the time they just ignored him, and went on their way. Some couldn't understand him when he did manage to get them to stop. He started to question his decision to come here in the first place. At home, people knew his name but here, he was of little or no importance.

At last, he spotted an old man, sucking on his pipe, which reminded him of his father. "Ubaba,"[53] he addressed the man, taking off his cap in respect.

"Yebo," came the reply.

"Can you please direct me to the mines? I am looking for work."

The old man had obviously heard this request many times before. He didn't answer, except to say, "Follow me."

That was more than enough for Fundile, so, case in hand,

---

[53] IsiXhosa for 'father'.

and cap back on his head, he followed the old man. It was already dark by the time the two got to the offices of the mine headquarters. The old man pointed to a sign that said, 'recruitment here'. Fundile had no idea what that meant, but he nodded. The old man spoke at last.

"Hambalala apha,"[54] was all he said, and disappeared into the night.

Fundile found a place to rest. Fortunately, he still had some of the food that his mother had packed some two days before. He ate what was left, made sure his suitcase was safely next to him, and then fell asleep.

The sun woke Fundile the next morning. He felt a little disorientated and immediately felt for his case and cap. Thankfully, they were still there. He then noticed that two other young men were already standing at the recruitment sign, so he got up and joined the queue. The other two men were from the Northern Cape and could speak his language. They told Fundile that they had been in the line yesterday, but the Umphathi[55] had only needed ten men that day and had told the rest to come again the following day.

At eight o'clock precisely, the doors opened and a White man and a Black man appeared. The White man said something, which Fundile only partly understood, but the Black man repeated the words in isiXhosa and isiZulu. By this time, the queue was twenty-deep at least. The first man in the line went in, and about three or so minutes later, the next man was called in. Now it was Fundile's turn. He stepped into the office and faced both men. Before they could speak, he removed his cap and said, "Good morning," just as the nuns had taught him.

---

[54] IsiXhosa for 'Sleep here'.
[55] IsiXhosa for 'boss man'.

"Good morning," replied the White man. "What is your name?"

"Fundile William Khumalo," he replied.

"Where do you come from?" smiled the officer.

"Kwagana, next to King Williamstown."

"Have you worked on a mine before?" asked the White man, and the Black man interpreted.

"No," answered Fundile, reaching for his precious certificate, and handing it to the White man. The recruiting officer took it, read it and smiled, then put the piece of paper on his desk. Fundile was very worried. That document was all he had, and he wanted it back in his pocket, not lying on the table!

"Well, this is an excellent document! We don't get many applicants with such a reference." Fundile had not heard the words 'documents' or 'reference' before, so he smiled. "You can start today," the White officer said, and the Black clerk translated into Fundile's home tongue.

A smile, as broad as the rising sun, showed on his face, and Fundile said, "Enkosi."[56]

"Go with Daniel, William," said the officer using Fundile's English name. "He will show you where you will sleep, eat and work." Fundile reached for his certificate. "No. We will keep this on your file." He had no idea what 'file' meant, so he smiled and followed the clerk.

Life in the workers' hostel, was a far cry from the life that Fundile, now William to the White miners, knew from home in his parents' kraal. Here, eight men shared a room. The beds were stacked two or three high, and the matrasses were made from hard coir, a dried hemp-like grass, but after a long day's

---

[56] IsiXhosa for 'Thank you'.

work, it was at least something to lie on. The food was sufficient but bland, and he longed for his mother's delicious cooking. In the evenings, each miner was given a big jug of 'Ibhiya,'[57] and by the time they had drunk the beer, the troubles of the day were soon forgotten, as was the hard mattress.

Fundile was good at his job, and his bosses had noticed that he was a cut above the others, intellectually, so they gave him a few wage increases. It was still much less than the White miners received, but a little more than the other Black miners. The authorities would have liked to raise Fundile's status at the mine, but they could not because of colour segregation. But that all changed in March 1922. There had been much fighting amongst the White miners during the previous few months. As far as Fundile understood, some of the White miners were concerned that the Black miners who worked for less would take over their jobs, even though there was a six-fold difference in their pay anyway.

These were difficult times, but Fundile got on with his work and hoped that the White miners would resolve their difficulties. However, on one particular day, he was told to report to the mine office, at the other end of the diggings. He was extremely worried, but he need not have been.

"William, we have noticed that you work very well and that your certificate states you passed standard two with English and arithmetic. We have decided to promote you to shift leader!"

---

[57] IsiXhosa word for 'a sorghum beer'.

Chapter 7

By now, the sunlight on the eastern façade of the church building had started to show its presence through the window pane, and a shaft of light was making itself known as it crept silently along the floor and up on to the pew where I was sitting.

Nothing could stop the sunray's march and it made me think of man's march on to his next set of circumstances. Some minor, some horrific like wars and famine, some just a change of residence, but whatever the case, it requires us to adapt to our new surrounds, and in some cases, rebuild our lives.

We study, we do our best to get ahead, we change our circumstances, and we strive to reach for the stars each day! Sometimes, more often than not, we do succeed, and our position on the ladder of hope rises a few steps.

At the time, when faced with choices, we make up our minds and pray that we have indeed made the right one. Only time, and that creeping beam of sunlight, will ever know the truth!

In 1918, the Treaty of Versailles was signed to mark the end of 'the war to end all wars'. Millions of soldiers had died on both sides, and so the world began to lick its wounds, and try and get back onto some sort of path of normality. South Africa had fortunately been spared the devastation of war damage, and it got back on its feet reasonably quickly. Soon, the gold mines on the Reef were operational again.

For the Porter-Smith family, it meant moving from Jeppestown to a more comfortable and leafier suburb on the northern outskirts of Johannesburg. In fact, they bought a farm in Edenburg, which was later to become Rivonia. It was not a working farm, but rather a gentleman's retreat! A river made its gentle way over gradual stones and rocks. A few horses roamed on the open veld and the beautiful sunsets could be seen over the mountains in the extreme west.

It was on one such summer's evening, that Michael's father asked him to join him on the veranda for a glass of white wine. "My boy," said his father. "Now that you have matriculated, it's time for you to think of your future studies. I have been giving it some thought, and I think that a degree from the University of the Witwatersrand will assist you in your future endeavours."

"Yes sir," was all Michael John could think of saying. This announcement had come as a shock. After all, he had just finished eight years at Jeppe School, not counting the years of home schooling and at another primary school; this was the time to start enjoying his life!

His father cut into his thoughts. "Well, Michael, what do you think of my idea?"

Michael knew that one did not argue with Mr Porter-Smith and got away with it easily. After all, his father had worked very hard to get where he was today. He had no formal education but through day-to-day slog, he had risen from a gold prospector to an agent, and then to a stake in an actual mine.

"Well, sir," Michael started, "I did quite well in accounting and mathematics at school, so I presume something in the world of commerce would be my forte."

"Good thinking, my boy! I thought along a similar line. I know the rector at the university. He and I are members of the Rand Club, so I will have a chat with him at next Friday evening's dinner."

"Thank you, Father." He was glad that the conversation was over for the time being.

The Christmas of 1918 soon came and went, and when 1919 burst into the world, humanity breathed a collective sigh of relief. Here was a new year, a new hope, a new beginning and with it came the opening of the new academic year at the universities and schools. Michael John's sisters started at Parktown Girls' School, and he started a three-year accounting degree at Wits.[58]

The next three years showed all sorts of growth. The bullion price rocketed to one hundred and thirty shillings per troy ounce. More and more cars were seen on the streets. The tram network, which started in 1906, was now extended, and trams were now even running in the upmarket northern suburb of Rosebank. Generally, the rich were getting richer, and the poor were, well, doing a lot of hard work!

Michael John attended lectures and progressed well. Lecture halls were mainly filled with young men, as accounting at this level was reserved mainly for males, while girls went to colleges, where they excelled at bookkeeping and secretarial activities. But, university and lectures only made up a third of the day and were limited to five days a week, so the rest of the time was for partying!

What better place was there to celebrate and party than at the Wanderers Club, just down the hill from the city centre, and

---

[58] An abridged name for the Witwatersrand University.

a walk away from Rosebank? Johannesburg had not escaped the flurry of the 1920 fashion rage, together with the 'wild' newly founded dance styles, and especially the dance bands pumping out the latest music.

Michael John had a comfortable trust fund, that his father would periodically top up. With his good looks and relative source of income, he had a string of eligible young ladies at his call. He wined and dined them, but by the time he qualified as a Chartered Accountant, in November 1921, a certain young lady had caught his attention.

Her name was Kathleen, but Michael John called her Betye. No one ever knew why he did, but she became Betye! She was different from all the other girls he knew. She had been born in the North Western part of the United Kingdom and had travelled to South Africa when she was still a young child. Her father was a prominent builder in Johannesburg, and the family lived in the suburb of Saxonwold, very near the zoo and the magnificent park.

Betye, herself, had a beautiful soprano voice, and in no time, she was offered the leading role with the Johannesburg Operatic Society. Michael John was hooked. This was the girl for him, and so he asked her to come to lunch at the farm in Rivonia to meet his parents and sisters.

Just one month later, the Rand rebellion, also known as the 1922 Strike, broke out, and within days, Johannesburg was a no-go zone. The trams and buses stopped running, and petrol was extremely difficult to obtain. Apart from the industrial unrest in the mining community, associated industries also joined in. Within weeks, economic depression slowly took hold, and the unrest spread quickly to other Reef towns, east and west of Johannesburg.

Eventually, as anarchy took hold, General Jan Smuts called up twenty thousand troops, including the Transvaal Horse Artillery and a first-world tank company. These troops crushed the rebellion, and a fragile peace was restored. But Jan Smuts would be blamed as the cause of the initial rebellion. White mine workers felt unprotected, and the call for colour segregation would again raise its ugly head!

Chapter 8

It is always a great and fascinating day when a new one is born into a family.

Before the child is a day old, the parents and the grandparents have already planned the outcome of the baby's life! But the significant wish, the unsaid prayer of the family, is that this child will not make the same mistakes as his or her parents made and that life would be fair to the newest member of the family.

The reality, though, is often different! Soon, the child will be introduced to the prejudices of the family, and their immediate circle. The chances of the new-born being able to make up his or her own mind are highly unlikely and almost impossible!

Society has a way of moulding a character into a complete clone of the person next door, and the person next door to that! Breaking out of the mould requires fortitude, resilience, daring and so often a promise of not returning to the train that relentlessly moves on.

Governments and people in authority know this trend, and make the most of the unwritten law, that very few people would even dare step over the line and show the establishment that they were wrong!

This sense of false security, by those in control, is exercised particularly by governments that are elected by the poor, uneducated majority!

Sarel junior was born exactly nine months after Sarel and Magdalien Van Wyk were married. This necessitated that Magdalien gave up her work at the YWCA so that she could take care of the baby. She had no family who could assist, and even though Sarel had sent a letter to his family in Van Stadensrus, his mother had replied, wishing them well, but no offer of assistance was forthcoming.

Fortunately, Sarel found out, that the railways did offer a slight increase in his weekly pay for each child in the family. This did help, and when he received that first pay increase, he went out and bought a bottle of brandy, and some of the new Coca-Cola that was now being imported into the country. He could not work out how it had taken so long for the soft drink to reach the Transvaal since it was first manufactured in 1892.

Dries (short for Andries) was born in 1924, just when the South African party, under Jan Smuts, lost to a coalition between the National Party, and the Labour Party, under J B Hertzog. This was a good day in Sarel's life. At last, the liberal English-speaking government would be replaced by a Nationalist government, even though they were still part of the Union of South Africa, and thus part of the British Empire! That thought still made Sarel's blood boil, and caused him to have another 'dop'.[59]

Two more births followed, one after the other, and Sarel applied to the railways for additional child funding. Magdalien looked so much older after each birth, and even though Sarel complained, she put on some extra weight after each birth and never lost it. Work was going well for Sarel, and he was promoted to boiler inspector. However, he felt more and more

---

[59] A drink of brandy and coke.

insecure, especially on the day that he heard that electric trains would soon be introduced on the Ladysmith line. His flat was now too small for six of them, and each time he walked to work, there were more and more Blacks on the streets.

In 1926, he was so glad to read an article in the South African Commercial advertiser, the local newspaper, that the new government had passed an Act in Parliament and a law, which enshrined White segregation and the so-called 'colour bar'.

Sarel and Magdalien's four children grew up, and fortunately, Sarel was offered a three-bedroom, heavily subsidised house, in a new railway housing development, just east of the Johannesburg city centre. Of course, he took it.

All was going reasonably well but in 1929, the world economy fell apart! Sarel read about it one night when he got home. Apparently, it had started in America, as he explained to Magdalien, and would soon spread to South Africa. With this news, Sarel poured himself another *dop*.

The Great Depression, as it would eventually be called, started when the gold standard, on which the West's economies relied, took a massive plunge and millions of people were put out of work, as stock exchanges closed their doors. In the same year, to add to the trauma, South Africa was dealt another blow – drought! The worst ever recorded. The impoverished walked the streets, looking for handouts.

The government did all it could. Those out of work were provided with menial labour, building dams and water canals – anything, just to feed a starving population. Sarel and his family were extremely fortunate. The South African Railways and Harbours (SAR&H) cushioned the blow by retaining their staff on an adjusted salary.

The arme wittes[60] population of South Africa had been born, and this was blatantly apparent in the city centre of Johannesburg. The once-thriving suburbs of Fordsburg, Doornfontein and Newlands, home to thousands of working-class families, had become White slums in just one year. In 1937, it was the City Council of Johannesburg's problem to resolve this issue, and they did so by establishing the new suburbs of Brixton and Brixton Ridge, not too far from where Sarel and his family lived. To qualify for a house in one of these areas, you had to be White and earn no more than twenty British pounds sterling per year, and many White families did.

The divide between the poor Whites, mainly Afrikaans speaking, and those living in the northern suburbs grew even deeper. Similarly, by now, to the northeast of the Witwatersrand, the township of Alexandra was now occupied by a Black majority. And so, the stage was set when in the early part of 1937, Hitler and his cohorts, became the talking point in the White areas. Anything but the English and the Brits!

Sarel, for one, had read about the Nazi movement, in the newspaper, and had often commented to Magdalien that he also approved of an Aryan race. During a similar article, Sarel had spotted that a group calling themselves Die Ossewa Brandwag,[61] established by a certain J F J van Rensburg in 1939, had offices based in Bloemfontein. Sarel very much liked what they stood for – Afrikaner nationalism. The group were decidedly anti-British, and pro-German.

The article reminded Sarel of the stories his father had told some thirty-nine years ago of how the British had rounded up

---

[60] Afrikaans for 'poor White'.
[61] Afrikaans for 'The Ox Wagon Brigade'.

Afrikaans (Boer) women and children and placed them in concentration camps, where many had died. J F J van Rensburg (Hans) explained the Fuhrer's principle of fighting against capitalists, communists and Jews and developing national socialism.

Sarel was so impressed by the article that he cut it out to keep for future reference. It wouldn't be long before he would read it again! In the early spring of 1939, Germany marched into Poland. England announced that they, and their allies, were formally at war with Germany and her allied forces. Immediately, in the colonies of Britain, South Africa was one of them, the debate arose as to whether or not they should join forces with Britain in their war effort.

Soon after, Sarel read that Australia, New Zealand and Canada would be sending their troops to join the British troops in their war effort. Sarel didn't sleep that night. The United Party, under J B Hertzog with his deputy Jan Smuts, were in control of the whole of South Africa, including Natal and the Cape Province, which were pro-British. Sarel wasn't surprised to hear that the Union of South Africa would be joining the war on the side of England, and would commission troops immediately. Sarel was eligible for a call-up, because of his age.

Sarel rushed home from work that afternoon, to discuss 'die hele gedoente'[62] with Magdalien.

"Hou 'n lae profiel,"[63] she had said to him. And that is what he did for the next week or so but, fortunately for Sarel, the call-up of White, Black and coloured soldiers was on a volunteer basis at that time. Thousands of eligible men and

---

[62] Afrikaans for 'the whole disastrous situation'.
[63] Afrikaans for 'Keep a low profile'.

women rushed to sign up, but Sarel was not one of them.

Instead, he went to his bedside drawer and dug out the newspaper article written about the pro-German *Ossewa Brandwag*. When Sarel knew that he would not be called upon to do active service, he verbally made it clear to his mates at work that he refused to enlist. Later that afternoon, he had signed up with the *Ossewa Brandwag*, and was known as a 'stormjaer'.[64]

He was given operations to carry out against the local servicemen, those who had volunteered, covertly, against any war effort. South African soldiers did get hurt, and many acts of sabotage were committed under the motto, "My God; My Volk; My Land, Suid Afrika!"[65]

---

[64] Afrikaans for 'storm hunter' or 'pathfinder'.
[65] Afrikaans for 'My God, My People; My Country, South Africa!'

Chapter 9

Fortunately, for the masses of a country, and particularly those with means, simple things like a secure place of employment, reasonable allowances and a full belly to go to sleep on are really the things that matter the most.

It would be madness to think that the masses don't have some desire to get out of the social, or poverty, hole in which they find themselves. Of course, they do, but for the most part, they are thankful for what they have, and for most of them, they enjoy a good night's rest, compared with those climbing the ladder to success, and who are easily knocked off, due to some uncalculated error!

The shaft of sunlight on my pew had now all but vanished, receding to the window from whence it had originated, indicating that the time was about ten o'clock and that I should really be joining the throng of businessmen and women working hard, and scraping together their wages for the day.

I couldn't get the thought out of my mind that even though the masses were reasonably happy with their lot, they still must think of a place, or a situation, that they could call home! Home – an institution whether you are rich or poor; home – a place where memories are made; home – where each of us can be exactly who we are; home – where hopefully each of us has a special place in the sun.

My mind turned to wartime refugees, the men, women and children, displaced by the horrors of conflict. Displaced people who were fleeing for their lives with what they had on their backs or in a basket. But these were not the refugees I had in mind at the time. My thoughts were for what I would call economic or financial refugees. Those who had to leave their homes to go far off to find work and, if they were exceptionally lucky, a fortune to make it all worthwhile. Those, of course, were few and far between!

Fundile had just celebrated his 26th birthday. He had accumulated some leave and had received a small Christmas bonus. Some of the smaller mines had been taken over by the bosses of his mine, and Fundile didn't understand what this meant, but often he had heard that some of his fellow hostel dwellers had lost their jobs, while others told of new mine shafts opening up.

Fundile hadn't ventured home for eight years now. When his wages permitted, he would send home a postal order, from the General Post Office. Only once, in all the years, did he hear, via a friend, that the family had received the money. So, he decided that this holiday time, he would make the long train journey home, to see his family.

Life in the mine hostel was not easy for Fundile and the others. The mine did provide basic food and a jug of sorghum beer, better known as Bantu Beer, each day, but the proximity of working shoulder to shoulder with your fellow miners and the rudimentary sleeping arrangements fuelled resentment between the Black miners and their White counterparts.

Fortunately, Fundile's basic education and his English language skills had helped him rise above the typical mine labourer. As each year passed, he could not help noticing that the mines were getting deeper and deeper, and the risk of following the gold reef or seam was getting more dangerous each day. There had been some tremors, and he had heard that some of his counterparts had been buried under rock falls.

It was time for Fundile to go home. He received his wages and his Christmas box[66] from the mine. He dug out his stash of saved money, packed it all in the right boot that he was wearing, and made his way to Park Station with his suitcase. His mind went back to that day when he had first arrived in Johannesburg.

At the ticket office, he asked for a third-class ticket to King Williamstown. At two o'clock that afternoon, the train pulled out of the station. It consisted of third-class[67], second and first-class coaches, with a dining car, and right at the back of the train was a goods van, which contained the excess first-class luggage.

This was truly a good day for Fundile! The fact that he couldn't lie down didn't bother him. He put his suitcase under his seat, where he could feel it, and he rested his head on the flat cap that the nuns had given him. He knew that his money was safe in his shoe, even though it hurt a bit. This was going to be a great holiday, and he could picture the surprise on the faces of his family, after all these years.

The train pulled into the King Williamstown station, four hours behind schedule, but this didn't worry Fundile. He disembarked, and couldn't help noticing that the station had changed in the last eight years. Once in town, he was amazed to see new buildings that had not been there before. Unperturbed, he walked along the main road, which eventually led to the open road leading to his home in Kwagana. The very thought of

---

[66] Annual bonus.

[67] Non-sleeping coaches.

his mother's cooking spurred him on, but even keeping a good pace, it would take him a few hours to get there.

He had been walking for about two hours when a horse-drawn wagon caught up with him. As it drew closer, he could see it was driven by a man, quite a bit older than he was. The wagon drew alongside him and Fundile removed his cap, and said, "Mholo."[68]

"Mholo," replied the driver, slowing the horses right down. "Uyaphi?"[69]

"Ekhaya,"[70] replied Fundile. "Kwagana." The driver stopped and invited Fundile to climb on the back. "Enkhosi Kakhulu,"[71] and soon they were trotting along.

Just outside Kwagana, the driver indicated that he was turning left, and Fundile saluted and jumped off, as he needed to go straight. He ran to the front of the cart, said, "*Enkhosi Kakhulu*" and lifted his cap as a sign of gratitude and respect.

He was now very near to his home, in fact about fifteen minutes away. The sun was setting, and being December, it set later than at other times. It was as if time had stopped, as he entered his parents' kraal. Nothing had changed in the eight years he had been away! One thing struck him though! Everyone was much older.

The greeting he received from his sisters was beyond crazy. They shouted and shouted, until his mother came rushing out, to see what all the noise was about. She stopped dead in her tracks and burst into tears. He ran the few metres to her and embraced her. Once she had stopped crying, she told him to come into the

---

[68] IsiXhosa word for 'Hello'.
[69] IsiXhosa for 'Where are you going?'
[70] IsiXhosa word for 'Home'.
[71] IsiXhosa for 'Thank you very much'.

house and greet his father.

Fundile wasn't prepared for what he found. His beloved, and much respected 'baba' seemed so old and frail. He lifted his head and smiled, and with wavering lips he said, "Unyana wam."[72] Fundile had brought gifts for each member of the family, which they were all delighted with. Thabile poured two jugs of home-brewed beer and gave one to Fundile and one to his father. The family gathered around, chatting about the years that had passed so quickly.

Early the next morning, Fundile asked his mother to come and talk to him privately. They found a comfortable spot under a tree in the yard. "*Umama*, I have also come home to find a wife. Can you tell me if Iviwe[73] is still unmarried?"

Thabile tried not to show too much emotion at his question. She replied, "No, my son, she is not married." She was tempted to tell him that Iviwe often asked after him. She lived two kraals away, and the two had often played together as children. Thabile also knew that Iviwe used to visit Fundile on the hills when he was watching the cattle and goats.

"Good!" smiled Fundile. *Good*, he thought to himself with relief. He had just over two weeks to seek her out and start the marriage procedure. Later that afternoon, he excused himself from his family and armed with a small gift, he went in search of her.

In true Xhosa tradition, Fundile had to go through the rites of a customary marriage, and that meant that he had to arrange for the elders (uncles and others who knew him well), to start the negotiation process of lobola.[74] These men would visit

---

[72] IsiXhosa for 'My son'.
[73] IsiXhosa name meaning 'Prayers have been heard'.
[74] IsiXhosa word mean 'dowry'.

Iviwe's father, and his assembled delegation, known as the Oonozakuzaku, who would negotiate the terms of the *lobola*. This was always done at the bride's home, and Fundile was not allowed anywhere near the negotiations.

In light of Fundile's short time at home, the negotiations had to be sped up, and on the day of the meeting, izibizo[75] of blankets, shawls for the women, hats, walking sticks and beer pots for the men were provided for the bride's family. After days of negotiating, the *lobola* for Iviwe was set at four cows or the cash equivalent. Fundile did not have four cows, but he did have many shillings stuffed into his boot, so he paid the *lobola* in cash, and the wedding took place at Iviwe's family kraal.

And so, it was a very sad day when later Fundile waved goodbye to his family and Iviwe, and set off on the long walk to the train station in King Williamstown. He smiled as he left. It had been a good few days at home, and he had added a wife to his family. She would help Thabile with the housework, and Fundile would send money home each month. It was also sad because he didn't know whether he would see his father again. Just before going over on the other side of the hill, he waved for the last time and went on his way.

The next few years at the mine seemed to grind away. Fundile stayed on at the mine hostel. Days were filled with the daily toil, but nights seemed long, and the beer became bitter in his mouth. He sent money home each month, with no guarantee that the family would receive it.

One afternoon, as he was coming off from his shift, an induna,[76] beckoned the younger man to come to him. It so

---

[75] IsiXhosa word for 'gifts'.
[76] IsiXhosa word for 'older, respected man'.

happened that this *induna* lived a mile or so from Fundile's family, and had recently been home. Fundile went over to the man, and he could see the tiredness in his eyes. They found a place to sit, and the old man started to tell his story.

He had gone home about two months ago and had overstayed his allotted leave time, and now the mine bosses had told him that there was no more work on the mine. Apparently, several mines were closing down, as were businesses, and many men were now begging on the streets for work, and even for bread. Many of the migrant workers were being sent home, and this Induna had returned, to plead for work, as he had nothing to eat.

Fundile had no way of helping him. He had heard that the White bosses had been talking of a depression, and Fundile had made sure to keep his head down and work hard. He considered himself lucky! It was 1929!

"But, baba, what news of my family in Kwagana?" The old man shook his head and explained that Fundile's father had died peacefully; the family had buried him at the base of the main tree, just outside the kraal. The same tree near where Fundile's umbilical cord had been buried after his birth. The old man wiped his face and seemed to delay speaking. So, Fundile asked, "But tell me about the rest of my family!"

The old man at last smiled, and said, "Your family is well, and your wife has two children."

"Two children? But that is impossible!" Fundile was outraged. *One, possibly, but not two! Who had fathered the second child?*

The old man laughed, with only a few teeth showing on his gums. "Amawele! Amawele!"[77] Fundile couldn't believe his

---

[77] IsiXhosa for 'Twins! Twins!'

ears! The old man carried on, "Inkwenkwe encinci. Intombi encinci.[78] Khazimela[79] and Asiphesona."[80]

Fundile was speechless. He shook the old man's hand and thanked him, and then he turned and walked away. He didn't want the old man to see his tears.

The mine where Fundile worked managed to get through the hard times of 1929, and he was promoted again to junior shift boss, which meant some extra pay. This meant that he could go home every second or third year. This he did, and exactly nine months after the first of these visits, Iviwe produced another child, Langalethu,[81] and three years later, came another child, Bonga.[82] From the moment Bonga was born, her life, and that of the family, would change forever.

She was born without pigmentation. Bonga was an Albino. She had the features of a Xhosa child, but her skin was White, and her eyes were a light colour and would cause problems for her for the rest of her life.

Fundile didn't tell his co-workers about this fourth child, and he decided not to go home for a while. It was 1939 and in his grief over Bonga, he left the hostel one night and went to Alexandra Township, where he found himself a girlfriend, Mavis; well, that was her English name!

---

[78] IsiXhosa for 'Little boy, little girl'.
[79] IsiXhosa for 'Shine bright'.
[80] IsiXhosa for 'Gift from God'.
[81] IsiXhosa for 'Our son'.
[82] IsiXhosa for 'Give thanks'.

Chapter 10

So often, our worlds need a shaking up, just in case we get too complacent. At the time, things seem to be rough, and of course, we ask the question why?

At the end of it all, provided we are still alive, we can view the shake-up from a philosophical point of view.

Strangely enough, sometimes, but not always, the world is better off having learnt some valuable lessons, and now richer for the experience, can move on.

It has been said of an individual that success comes with a lot of hard work, and this is true. Wouldn't it be wonderful if all those who set out on a path of endeavour reaped the reward of success; this is not always the case, and many fall victim to failure.

But for me, as I sat there contemplating, I believed that some accolades – no! a lot of accolades, must surely go to those who at least try.

My blood pressure immediately started to rise, as I thought of those who don't even try, but are so quick to criticise, and even condemn those who make an effort. Isn't it the case when those who do try, fail, and those self-same people are the ones who say "I told you so!" How dare people, family and friends condemn those who give it a go! Without these adventures, we would still be living in caves!

I took a deep breath and adjusted my position on the pew. Just for a moment, I heard what sounded like the start of a shake-up, and my blood went cold. I realised that this time, it would take more than a while for the dust to settle!

It took many months to get Johannesburg, and particularly Reef towns like Brakpan and Benoni, back into shape after the 1922 miners' strike. There was much structural damage, but the damage to ordinary people's employment and finances was much more devastating.

Ordinary mine workers lost their jobs, and Black mine workers were either sent home to their homelands or even became replacements for White mine workers, as their pay package was less than that of White workers. However, life on the Reef eventually returned to normal, the state of the economy lifted, and the financial heartbeat of Johannesburg was soon pumping again.

In the new year, Michael John walked onto the campus of the University of the Witwatersrand to start his second year of study in the faculty of commerce and accounting. He had a smile on his face as he greeted his pals and other fellow students. He was elated, as he had passed the first year with distinction.

The students all chatted about their December holiday, what they had done, where they had gone, as well as their various love pursuits. Of course, they all spoke with bravado as to how they each would have solved the miners' strike. This inevitably sparked much debate, and by the time the group got to the lecture hall, there already had been some harsh words said. It took the professor a while to get the class to settle down.

Four years soon passed. They were great years for Michael John, and he obtained his commerce degree cum laude. That year, Michael John celebrated his twenty-sixth birthday, and as his father had said for the umpteenth time, it was time to find a responsible job. He drove from the farm in Rivonia, through Rosebank and into Johannesburg. On the corner of Eloff and Commissioner Streets, stood the newly built National Bank of South Africa. It was the bank's head office, and it held pride of place in the heart of Johannesburg's central district.

He parked his automobile, straightened his tie, combed his hair, and walked towards the main entrance of the bank. As he approached the elaborate door to the building, a newspaper boy handed him a copy of the day's paper and demanded a 'tickey'.[83] Michael felt in his pocket and handed the youngster the silver coin, then he pushed open the door and walked into the bank.

The young lady at reception smiled at him and unwittingly adjusted the combs in her hair. She was wearing a crisp, white blouse and a long brown skirt. "Can I help you?" she asked politely.

"Please," replied Michael. "I have an appointment with Mr Osborn at ten o'clock." He took out his pocket watch and checked the time. It was exactly 9.55 a.m.

"Make yourself comfortable over there," she said, indicating a table with three chairs around it. He did as he was asked, and the receptionist walked off down a passage. She was aware that he was watching her every move.

Michael took this opportunity to look through the paper he had just bought. He glanced at the headlines – just the usual stuff. Racial discrimination was headlined again. There was a sub-title about a White House issue, and another that spoke of the gold price rising again at the Johannesburg Stock Exchange

---

[83] A South African coin that was worth about three cents.

(JSE) and that commercial banks were making loans available to suitable clients at 3% interest. He made a note of this. He could perhaps use it to his advantage in the interview.

The receptionist soon returned and walked over to where he was sitting. He folded the paper and stood up politely. "Mr Osborn will see you now. Please follow me." She tried her best not to blush, as he looked her up and down. He followed her down a rather long corridor, and they eventually arrived at a door that was marked 'Personnel Manager'.

She knocked on the door and opened it when told to enter. She stepped in and said, "Your ten o'clock appointment, sir. This is Mr Porter-Smith." Michael stepped into the office and she left, closing the door behind her.

"Good morning, Mr Osborn. Thanks for seeing me." Michael John extended his hand to shake that of the older man.

"Good morning, Mr Porter-Smith. I see you are here looking for employment." The interview that followed went very well. Michael John showed all his university credentials and some letters of reference that his father had organised from the right people. As the interview drew to a close, the personnel manager told him that he could have the position of junior investment banker if he was prepared to do a six-month bankers' training course. This meant that he would start off counting money, as a teller, and then move on to calculating interest levies and customer accounts.

There was no actual discussion about salary, as these were based on a scale, as prescribed by the top echelon of bankers, based here at head office. "Well, what do you think? The position is yours if you want it."

"Thank you, sir. I would be very happy to accept the position." The manager went on to tell him to come in the next day, to start his training.

When he got up, Mr Osborn saw that Michael had the newspaper, and he said, "Terrible business about the Whites in the slums. I wonder what the politicians are going to do about sorting out the problems between the Whites and the Blacks?"

Michael did not want to get into a political conversation, so he just said, "I'm glad it is not my problem!"

"Well said!" came the reply. "Let me pass on these words. Never forget them as long as you live. Money rules everything; don't forget that! Well, good day, Mr Porter-Smith, we'll see you at eight, sharp, in the morning!"

Michael shook the man's hand, thanked him, and left the office. That night, there was a party at the farm to celebrate, and Betye was also invited.

Michael's career in the bank went from strength to strength. Typical bank bureaucracy did get him down sometimes, and when he threatened to leave, Betye persuaded him to keep working hard, which he did, and by the time the big depression of 1929 came, he held the position of Investment Manager.

He was indeed grateful every morning, as he walked to work. He would pass so many men and women, both Black and White, standing in queues waiting for soup and bread, and anything else being handed out. He soon learned not to wear fancy clothes to work, because they were like a magnet to hungry, out-of-work people, who sat on the pavements, and on street corners in Johannesburg's city centre.

Fortunately, because of his work in the bank, Michael saw the start of money flowing through the system once more, and as he said to his family and Betye, this would bring to an end the horrible depression. So, the worldwide depression did end, but it had taken its toll on many businesses that collapsed, dreams that were shattered and various racial groups who were relocated. On the other hand, it taught lessons of reconsolidation and better financial standards, and it gave Michael the expertise he needed, as the manager of investments, at the National Bank of South Africa.

On a particular Saturday afternoon, Michael John and Betye were walking along the river on the Rivonia farm, when he asked for her hand in marriage. She, of course, said "Yes" and they were married in December 1930 in a little church in Parktown. All their friends and family attended the marvellous affair, and after a honeymoon in Durban, the couple returned to a lovely house they had purchased in the suburb of Parkhurst, a short walk from the bus station in Rosebank. This suited them, as they were both now working in Johannesburg.

Three very happy years followed, with Michael completely involved with investors, trying to get their share of the property market, particularly that of the so-called 'Jan Hofmeyer Improvement Scheme' and sub-economic township development for the poor Whites.

This major township development for Whites was to be to the west of Johannesburg, in an area called Roodepoort. Meanwhile, to the southwest of Johannesburg, the government was establishing a temporary neighbourhood, for the Black gold miners, called South Western Township (Soweto). Michael found that there was no appetite for investors for the Soweto Project. But as the Alexandra Township, to the northeast, filled up, so Soweto started to gain momentum.

The banks did lend money, and the investors saw a great return on their investments. Johannesburg and the Union of South Africa grew, even if it was with White South Africans, supporting Hertzog or Smuts, depending on the ebb and flow of their policies, or the Blacks, who supported the African

National Congress, which had its original roots in the Eastern Cape.

Peter Henry was born to Michael John and Betye in the autumn of 1939. Life carried on for that family, as it did for others, but in September of that year, the clouds of war gathered, and Britain declared war on Germany on 3 September. There was much debate in South Africa as to whom the country should support. It went to a populous vote; General Jan Smuts defeated Hertzog, and South Africa was at war with Germany and her allies. There was much talk amongst the English-speaking people who were concerned that the Afrikaans-speaking people would sabotage the war effort in favour of the Nazis. This enforced the commitment of many brave young South Africans who signed up to go to war.

Michael John was amongst the first to put their name down at the recruitment office in Auckland Park, a suburb in the heart of Johannesburg. Soon, regiments like the South African Irish Regiment, the Transvaal Horse Artillery, the ILH (Imperial Light Horse), Transvaal Scottish, and so many others, were mustered and shipped off to East Africa, and then on to North Africa, and finally, fighting to liberate Italy.

Both White and Black men volunteered. The Black soldiers were mainly in a non-combatant, but supportive roll. Michael John quickly got rank, and this meant that he could send money home to Betye and their son, Peter. Sadly, Michael was wounded in the Battle of El Alamein, at Tobruk in North Africa, and was sent home to recover.

The second world war was won; Michael John healed and went back to work at the bank. The years between 1939 and 1945 brought massive changes to the economic and political landscape of South Africa.

Chapter 11

I got up from the pew and realised that it had become very warm in the church, so I went to the nearest window and unlatched it. As I opened it, there was an immediate rush of cool air that breezed in, and it brushed against my face as it passed.

I scolded myself for not opening the window earlier. Perhaps the fresh air would have made me think differently. Maybe I could have avoided some of the despair that was still to come!

"Where is the new beginning?" I kept saying to myself. "How much will it take to heal the wounds that the past few years have brought?"

I left the window fully open and returned to what had become my favourite pew.

Along with the fresh air that was steadily blowing through the now-open window came the chatter of birds, and, possibly, the sound of the odd beetle. I paused for a while, and realised that the birds and the beetles were trying to out-chatter, out-chirp or whatever birds and beetles do, to get someone's attention!

Possibly it was just wishful thinking, but I thought I could hear them saying,

"Listen to me! I have the loudest voice!"

"This is the way we should get things done!"

"Follow me, I have the best plan, don't listen to others!"

"Rubbish!" I said to myself. "I can make up my own mind!"

The end of the war saw great relief for the families of soldiers returning home, but also much hardship. The lucky ones, who were in the minority, had jobs and businesses to go back to, but the greater majority had nothing.

Employment was scarce, development was slow and investments were rare. Those returning from war were desperate, and Field Marshal Jan Smuts, the prime minister, made promises, but the population soon turned against him. A major election was needed, and it needed to happen soon! But the election date was only scheduled for 1948.

The Blacks had technically lost their voting rights, with some exceptions. The war years had seen to it that this did not gain much prominence, and they were now competing equally on the labour market for almost non-existent employment.

In Sarel's household, he and his wife, and four children, were doing reasonably well. The railways had rewarded him with a promotion of five extra days added to his annual leave, and a better pension. He was convinced that this was because his boss in the engineering department had seen him at an anti-war rally, held in a dimly lit hall in Joubert Park.

Sarel's children had been enrolled in primary school, near their home, so it was easy for the four children to walk to school each day. Children had to wear a school uniform, which Petronella bought from a government-subsidised uniform shop, at a marginal price, but regulation school shoes were another matter, as these were not subsidised, resulting in many of the children going to school barefoot (without socks and shoes.)

Despite the bumpy start to the work situation, the South

African economy started to see a rebirth, so much so that in 1947 ,the British Royal family came to visit the country and spend time holidaying. While crowds thronged the streets, and waved the Union Jack, Sarel and his family, and a lot of others, boycotted the parades and celebrations. There was too much work required to set the Afrikaners free!

In 1948, Sarel, and most of South Africa, went to the polls to cast their votes. Sarel had received a letter the week before, from his coloured Aunt Flo, asking if Sarel felt that she should vote. He quickly disposed of the letter, before Petronella could see it, and ask any questions about his family.

Sarel knew that all coloureds and Asians could vote, but he wasn't going to tell his aunt that. It even annoyed Sarel that some specific Blacks were allowed to vote, albeit for seven White parliamentarians. Nonetheless, Sarel and his wife, and all their friends, went to the polling station to cast their vote. The choice was simple. Either vote for the existing South African Party, the Herenigde[84] National Party, the Labour Party, or a few independents that were standing for election.

Sarel's choice was easy. He would not vote for that bloody Jan Smuts, who had supported the war effort those years before. He also would not vote for the Labour party, or the individual independents, as most of them were Englishmen anyway. So, he voted for the HNP and was delighted when they won the election, and Dr D F Malan was sworn in as the Prime Minister of the Union of South Africa. The new government went into session, and apartheid[85] was born. The peoples of South Africa were separated according to their race. White minority rule was entrenched, and the discrimination of non-White people was

---

[84] Afrikaans word for 'Reunited'.
[85] Afrikaans word for 'Apartness'.

written into law.

Sarel and his cronies were delighted! Field Marshall Smuts was history! Sarel's job was secure, and he and his children no longer had to compete with non-Whites for positions of work or school space. Sarel celebrated with his favourite *dop* of brandy and coke.

Surprisingly, the world did little to object. Most countries were busy restoring their economies to pre-war levels, or they were frantically rebuilding their broken infrastructures. Anyway, South Africa was thousands of kilometres away, so who cared, if just two years later, the mouthpiece of the South African Blacks, the ANC, was banned forever!

For Sarel, this all meant nothing. The Blacks, coloureds and Asians were still pouring into Johannesburg and other big cities, selling their labour at prices the White population could, or couldn't, compete with. Soweto and Alexandra were growing exponentially, and Sarel felt that his job was threatened, even though the whole of South Africa was experiencing a massive growth boom!

Sarel agitated, his friends agitated, people in the housing complex agitated, and the government of D F Malan heard. So, they passed the *Group Areas Act 41 of 1950,* in terms of which one had to live in specified areas. Whites lived in White areas, and Blacks were not allowed to enter a White area without a dompas[86] – a document signed by a white person and stamped by an official at the 'pass office', where one had to apply for the particular non-White to be allowed into the area.

And so, the pass system was adopted. Sarel was surprised to read that this was nothing new. In 1760, passes were put in place to keep the slaves out of the White areas. At last,

---

[86] Afrikaans for 'dumb passport'.

something tangible had been done that Sarel could understand. Each non-White, over the age of sixteen, had to carry a signed pass. At work, it became Sarel's task to sign these passes, allowing the workers to enter Johannesburg each day to attend their jobs.

Petronella had to do the same thing for her ironing 'girl'[87] (maid) who came to work for her each Wednesday, allowing her to travel from Soweto to Johannesburg. On occasion, Petronella was otherwise occupied, so Sarel junior signed the pass as he was now over sixteen. Sadly, the ironing lady was old enough to be his mother!

Dr D F Malan was replaced by Prime Minister J G Strijdom. Sarel was sad to see Malan go, but he had high hopes for the more right-wing Strijdom, who would be put to the test, as he read in the papers one Sunday while relaxing at home. Black women were agitating for the transformation of social conditions, and had threatened to march to the Union Buildings, the seat of government, in Pretoria.

Strijdom ignored their pleas, and as a result, twenty thousand Black, coloured, Indian and some White women marched to the Union Buildings and handed over a petition to the government, insisting on the cancellation of the pass law!

Sarel was relieved to report to his colleagues that Strijdom was not interested in the pleas of the women marchers. At home, Petronella took pride in signing her ironing girl's pass and insisted that they now only converse in Afrikaans.

---

[87] Common term for maid, irrespective of their age.

Chapter 12

It's true to say that each of us is never really satisfied with what we have, and because of this, we venture out and live a little on the edge! It keeps the adrenalin pumping and gives us a feeling of being invincible. Generally, this is a purely natural state of mind, and it motivates us to get out of our comfort zone and press forward and onward to new adventures.

As we take a cautious step into the unknown, we do rely on the safety net of our families, our homes our employment, and of course, our health. Each one of these is essential, and if one of these fails, our journey forward is in jeopardy.

Suddenly, all that our lives stood for and those whom we love seem but a distant memory. New faces appear in our lives, and we are forced to trust them, even though they are total strangers at the time of our fall! New surrounds become the dominant features, and what we called home soon becomes just an illusion of what was.

Just when things seem to reach an all-time low, and the entire world seems to strangulate the last bit of hope out of you, literally out of the blue, comes a guardian angel, and the chaos that has been yours for a while miraculously goes away!

World War II came and went, as far as Fundile was concerned, he and the other miners were not involved, and it hadn't affected them too much. In truth, they all worked a little harder, as some of their bosses had gone off to fight in another country.

This became the talk in the mine hostel at night.

During those five or so years, Fundile went home twice. He sent money regularly, and the news he got from home was generally good. Iviwe was fine, the children were doing well at school, but Bonga was being teased unmercifully by the other children, and so she didn't go to school on occasion. His head of cattle was growing, and Thabile was selling quite a lot of milk, and every so often, she would sell off a bull.

Fundile was, however, visiting Mavis in Alexandra quite regularly, and she was keeping him satisfied. Each Friday, after his shift ended, Fundile would catch a Putco[88] bus and make his way to Alexandra Township, where he would stay with Mavis for the weekend. But, in December 1945, the residents of Alexandra decided to boycott the Putco bus service, and instead, they walked to Johannesburg, to their places of employment. Fundile soon learnt that this was because the bus company had put up the prices of the fares, which had annoyed the residents. Fundile joined the walkers for a few weeks but soon tired of it, deciding not to visit Mavis until the bus company and the residents had come to an agreement. They did, and he was soon knocking on Mavis's door once again.

The days underground were monotonous and tiring, but one night, after Fundile had eaten, and had his jug of beer, he went to his room and climbed into his bunkbed. It wasn't particularly cold, but he could not get warm, and he battled with a niggling cough the whole night. The next day, while underground, he again felt cold, even though the temperature in the mine shaft was normally above average, and he shivered and coughed persistently.

That night, he didn't sleep at all and eventually went to sit

---

[88] Public Utility Transport Company.

outside, so that he would not disturb his fellow hostel-dwellers. At eight o'clock the next morning, he reported to the mine's sick bay, where the sister examined him, and then sent him, with a piece of paper, to see the mine doctor. The doctor didn't have to be a genius. He had seen it before. Fundile had TB.[89] The doctor explained that he would have to go away for many months from his work and that he could seek help from the TB Hospital in Rietfontein, east of Johannesburg, not far from Alexandra Township.

The doctor told him that he was first to report to the mine office with the doctor's report, on which he seemed to be scribbling. Once in his hand, Fundile took the report to the mine office and gave it to the Lungu[90] boss, Mr E Smit. Smit knew Fundile well and they greeted one another; Fundile gave him the report from the doctor. Immediately, Smit moved backwards and covered his nose and mouth with his hands.

"Fundile, you are very sick! You must go to the hospital in Rietfontein today. We do not want the other workers to become ill! Go and fetch all your things, and meet me here in one hour. I will get your back-pay organised. Take everything, but leave your helmet, lamp and battery pack."

Fundile turned and walked out of the office, and went to the hostel. He was confused. He didn't know what was wrong with him, and why Boss Smit had told him to go! Had he done something wrong? Worst of all, he had no idea where the Rietfontein Hospital was! Fortunately, his hostel mates had gone off to their shift, so he packed his meagre possessions, put on his going-out clothes, and best shoes, and made sure that the doctor's letter was in his pocket. He folded his overalls, and

---

[89] Tuberculosis.
[90] IsiXhosa word for 'White'.

blankets, and left them on his bed with the helmet and lamp. There was no one to bid farewell to, so he took his things and went back to the mine office.

Smit and the clerk were waiting for him. The boss handed a packet to him, which he didn't even check. He trusted Smit after all these years. "Yiya Ngokekhselekileto,"[91] said Smit, and he walked back into his office. Fundile asked the clerk where Rietfontein Hospital was and he explained to Fundile how to get there. Fundile walked off the mine property for the last time.

He spent two and a half years at the TB Hospital. He had tried to contact Mavis, who was only four kilometres away, in Alexandra township, but she ignored him. He was lucky enough to get a message to Iviwe, and his family in Kwagana. He had used up all the money that had been in his last pay packet, and he wondered how his family would survive.

The hospital staff were very kind. His coughing had got progressively worse, and he lost a lot of weight, especially muscle. After about eighteen months, he started to feel a bit better, and he was allowed to join the other patients on the lawns of the property; after the end of the second year, he was encouraged to do some handwork with the others in a shed in the hospital grounds.

He soon learnt to weave and to make leather-thong shoes, and one of the sisters had helped him to improve his reading. At last, after thirty months, he was declared fit, and was allowed to leave the hospital, which had become a safe haven! He had no idea where to go. Mavis wasn't an option, and with no money, he couldn't go home!

The hospital gates closed behind him, and he didn't know whether to turn left to Johannesburg or right to Alexandra. He

---

[91] IsiXhosa for 'Go Safely'.

hadn't gone very far when a police van pulled up, and a voice shouted, "Hey swarte! Waar gaan jy?"[92]

Fundile had learnt a smattering of Afrikaans in his time at the mine, but he replied in English, "To Alexandra."

"Waar is jou pass?"[93] demanded the constable. Fundile had no idea what the policeman was asking, so he shrugged and said nothing. "Waar is jou pass?" the man asked again, more insistently. When he got no response, he got out of the van and walked over to Fundile, and pushed him towards the van. He opened the back door of the van and beckoned for Fundile to climb in.

There were three other Black men in the van, and Fundile greeted them politely. They were surprised when they heard Fundile's silence when asked about his pass. He explained to the men that he had been in hospital for nearly three years and didn't know what a pass was. They quickly explained to him, and Fundile couldn't believe what he was hearing. Why did he have to get permission to walk in a White area? It had never been like that before!

The one prisoner in the van had obviously been in this same position before, so he explained to Fundile what to do when his case came before the magistrate. Once in court, he pleaded guilty, and explained about his long stay in the hospital and that he had been unaware of the new law to carry a pass. The magistrate just smiled, and banging his gavel said, "Go! Get a passbook from the clerk on your way out!"

Fundile found the clerk, who wrote his name and date and place of birth, in the book, and told him to get his White boss to sign the book, or he was to go home, immediately. He took the

---

[92] Afrikaans for 'Hey, Black man. Where are you going?'
[93] Afrikaans for 'Where is your pass?'

book and put it in his top pocket. He didn't have a boss, and he didn't have money to go home, so he turned to walk to Alexandra.

This time, a little fortune smiled on him. He was about three kilometres away from Alexandra, when another van, this time with an open back, pulled up next to him. "Hey, you!" said the voice from the cab. The man spoke English.

"Yes, baas!" replied Fundile.

"Do you want to come and do some garden work for me?" asked the driver.

"Yes, please baas!" said Fundile, gratefully. By now he was very tired, not having walked this far for the last few years. He had no idea how he would work in a garden, but it was at least a chance to make some money, and perhaps he would get something to eat.

"Climb on the back," said the voice, and Fundile threw his belongings onto the back of the van, and he climbed aboard. The van sped off in the direction of Edenvale, that is what was written on the signboard they passed. That chance meeting on the roadside continued for nearly ten years. The MacDonalds lived in Edenvale, in a four-bedroomed house, with a huge garden and a private stable that housed two horses.

Fundile, ever quick at learning, took up the position as gardener and soon learnt the do's and don'ts of gardening from Mrs MacDonald. His employment included meals, cooked by Lily, the house maid, and he had a khaya[94] in the garden, with a shower and a toilet. This was a kind of heaven to him!

His strength grew day by day, and after two months in the employ of the MacDonalds, he was again able to start sending money home, via the post office. A week or so, after sending

---

[94] IsiXhosa for 'home' or 'room'.

that first money home, he was very surprised to receive a letter addressed to him. Mrs MacDonald called him and gave him the letter that had been delivered to their house. He had never received a letter before, so he carefully opened the envelope, and unfolded the piece of paper.

It was from his son, Khazimela, one of the twins. Fundile was delighted, and though his reading ability was limited, he went and sat down, and read the letter. Everything at home was going fine, according to Khazimela. Fundile's mother, Thabile, was a little frail, but okay. Iviwe was still working hard, and the head of cattle had grown substantially.

Khazimela went on to report that they had heard from one of the miners, who had visited his home, that Fundile was sick, and that is all they knew, and they were worried about him. He thanked him that they had started receiving money again, and by this, they assumed that he was well again. Khazimela had obtained the MacDonalds' address, from the deposit slip, received from the post office.

Fundile was so happy, and tears were streaming down his face. The letter continued. Khazimela explained that he was now eighteen years old, and had done well at school. He had enrolled at the University of Fort Hare, at Alice, in the Eastern Cape. Fundile read that part again. Where would he find the money for this tuition?

The answer came in the next paragraph. Khazimela said that if they sold three or four of the cattle, that would be enough for him to go to university. He concluded the letter by asking his father's permission to do this.

Fundile put the letter back in its envelope and walked to his khaya, and sat down to think. This was a huge request! A big day in his life! An hour later, Mrs MacDonald called him, and he went back to work. He toiled in the garden until it was time to finish for the day. He decided that he would speak to Mr MacDonald when he came home from work.

He waited for his boss to park his Ford in the garage, and go into the house. He waited another ten minutes, and then he went to the back door, and asked Lily to call the master. "Hey wena![95] What do you want with the baas?"

"Please just call him. I want to speak to him." She turned to leave the kitchen in search of Mr MacDonald. Surprisingly, both Mr and Mrs MacDonald appeared at the door!

"Good evening, Fundile. How can we help you?"

Fundile tried, in his best English, to ask for their opinion on Khazimela's request. Mr MacDonald lit a cigarette and looked at the man standing in front of him. He reckoned that Fundile was about his own age. Although Fundile had not worked for them for that long, the reports he got from his wife were very favourable, and she also reported that he was very willing and polite. He took another draw on his cigarette, and said, "Fundile, or is it better to call you William?"

Fundile stood there, twisting his cap in his hands, while waiting for an answer.

"I think it is an excellent plan!" He noticed the broad smile on the man's face. He went on, "But it is a lot of money to pay for university for three years." He noticed the immediate look of disappointment on the other man's face. "If you promise to work hard, and listen to everything we tell you, I will try and arrange a bursary for your boy through my company."

The look of disappointment immediately turned into one of consternation. He did not understand what bursary meant and looked at Lily for an isiXhosa explanation because he knew she

---

[95] IsiXhosa for 'you'.

was listening to the conversation. There was no explanation forthcoming. Instead, Mr MacDonald said, "I will help you each month, to get the money for the university. Ask your son for the details of Fort Hare, and I will do the rest." He made a note to speak to the other board members and fill them in, as to whom they could give their first bursary.

"What is your son's name?"

"Khazimela Khumalo," came the reply. "Thank you, my baas! Thank you!"

MacDonald kept his word, and each month, a cheque would be mailed to the university for the boy's tuition. Fundile continued to work in the garden, which flourished as a showpiece, and he got to go home each Christmas. Mrs MacDonald had signed his passbook so many times that she had to go to the Government Pass Office, a few times, to renew his book and Lily's too. As the years passed, his English improved too.

One day, while planning a new rose garden with Mrs MacDonald, she asked him what he thought about the women marching to Pretoria to have the pass law abolished. He replied openly that it hurt him every time he walked to catch the Putco bus, or go to the shop, that he was stopped by a policeman demanding his pass. He explained that he came from the Eastern Cape, and no one cared if you walked in the White man's area!

In 1958, things changed dramatically for Fundile. He and Lily had spoken about the forthcoming general elections. They didn't have the vote anyway, but Khazimela had visited his father recently and had explained the process to them both. The boy had graduated from Fort Hare with distinction in political studies and human sciences. He had come to thank the MacDonalds for their help. As they discussed the elections, Lily said that she had overheard the *missus*[96] say that J G Strijdom had died, and that is why the voting had to take place.

During September of 1958, the house in Edenvale was very busy with visitors, some coming very late at night. Big black cars had come, some even had chauffeurs, and the house lights would remain on well into the night. Eventually, one night, according to Lily, a Makhulu baas[97] had arrived, by the name of Sir De Villiers Graaf. She remembered because she had served tea to the man and her boss.

Election Day came, and ballots were cast; the National Party under the leadership of Dr Hendrick Verwoerd won, defeating the United Party, yet again. Fundile and Lily's time at the house in Edenvale came to an end, as Mr MacDonald had won a seat in the Cape Town Parliament, and the family had to relocate. They were both paid handsomely for their service, with leave pay and a good bonus.

---

[96] South African term for 'madam'.
[97] IsiXhosa for 'big important boss'.

Chapter 13

Without notice, the orchestra of chirping birds, and the sounds of crickets or bugs, suddenly stopped. The break in the sound was almost deafening! So much so that I lost my train of thought!

I turned to look at the open window to see what was going on, and my question was answered immediately. A cat had jumped up onto the window ledge, and this furball was trying to make its way into the church. I did what I thought was correct, and made the only cat noise that I could think of. "Pss! Pss!" I said, and to my absolute surprise, the cat understood my cat language, and it hopped from the window sill and onto my lap!

I was delighted as I adore cats, and so I made a fuss of the visitor. She preened herself, arched her back, and started to knead my legs with her claws. Cats do that sort of thing, so it did not annoy me. I continued to stroke the cat, and she must have known that I was friendly, because she curled up on my lap and simply went to sleep.

This little interlude had upset my train of thought, and I decided that the world would progress onwards, regardless of what my new furry friend did, or thought!

Michael John was one of the lucky ones! He had a solid job to come back to after the war, and after he had healed. The bank pay was minimal, but unlike a lot of others, it did put food on the table and paid the rent.

As the year 1946 dawned, the economy started to lift and would continue to do so for the next thirteen years. Life in Parkhurst was good; Peter Henry grew and blossomed at school. He was transferred to a private boys' school, which put a bit of strain on the family's resources, but they had decided that education was all important, and they were prepared to sacrifice other luxuries in order for their boy to get a good education.

Betye, who always had a secret liking, and flair, for politics, worked hard for the South African Party, supporting and admiring Field Marshall Jannie Smuts. The party workers held numerous raffles and cake sales, as well as concerts, which were Betye's speciality, to raise funds for the party. Sadly, in 1948, the South African Party lost to the HNP of D F Malan. The loss was a political blow for Betye's party of choice, and it heralded everything evil. It was very anti-English-speakers.

The emphasis shifted dramatically from the centre and left to the complete right wing! To keep itself in power, the HNP would further smother the political aspirations of the Black people, so much so that just two years later, the only mouthpiece of the Black people, the ANC, would be banned forever.

Yet, in those years, the economy boomed. The gold standard broke all records; the downtown clubs and theatres of Johannesburg swayed to the music of the big bands; sales of automobiles rocketed and the English-speaking part of the community did their own thing. Some politically associated women formed objector groups, standing on street corners and waving banners each time the National government passed another racial law. In Johannesburg, the English-speaking majority still held the purse strings. The Union of South Africa was still a British colony, and the British Empire still ruled, no matter what the local government said. This fact had been fortified by a visit of the royal family.

Michael John and Betye decided this would be a good time to increase their family, so in 1949, another son, David, was born. The house in Parkhurst was declared too small, and the family decided to move the entire household to a fairly newly established suburb, still in the northern area, called Orchards. The area offered a suitable primary school in the older, adjacent suburb of Norwood. Conveniently, there was an Anglican church down the road from the house, and a huge Dutch Reformed church, nearby, where on a Sunday, single-decker buses would arrive with Afrikaans-speaking people, who would enjoy the worship service, and then be taken home again.

Alexandra Township was about ten kilometres away, so gardeners and maids could make their way to work each day if they didn't live on the property. In these northern suburbs of Johannesburg, the South African party, soon to become the United Party, flourished, and Betye would become more and more involved with the affairs of the party. It seemed that Johannesburg was politically divided, not completely, but divided into the northern and the southern suburbs. The social barrier between the North and the South was often a discussion point.

The Party stalwarts in the Orchards/Norwood area, among them, Betye, would arrange jumble sales of second-hand clothing; cake sales; raffles, anything that would raise the coffers of the party to help fight the next election.

At the other end of the scale, the HNP under the leadership of J G Strijdom were deadly serious in their mindset of Blanke baasskap[98] at all costs. This policy was to be the cornerstone of all the HNP policies. The mainly Afrikaans-speaking electorate supported Strijdom, to the extent that a major street was to be named after him!

The party organised the cancellation of the coloured voter's roll, thus disenfranchising the entire coloured population from voting. The electorate cheered, and named a new suburb, Strijdom Park, after him. The United Party held yet another book sale, and later that year it became politically clear that the HNP was moving areas to sever all ties with the British Monarchy. This announcement was again received with peals of joy from the right wing, and when a tunnel was constructed in the Eastern Transvaal, it was named after J G Strijdom. The United Party had another cake sale to raise funds.

But the year 1956 would be a trying one for Strijdom and his government. The ladies of the United Party had got wind of the march to Pretoria, being organised by Black women in protest of the pass laws, and some of their members decided to join the Black women in their march. These ladies organised for the Star and Sunday Times newspapers to take pictures and cover the protest, little knowing that these pictures and articles would be preserved for posterity. Unfortunately, this march only cemented the resolve of the ruling party to tighten their *Blanke baasskap*.

But 1956 would bring a much more crippling, and potentially dangerous, situation into the realm of the government seats. The party realised that because of the protest march, the Blacks, with the gathering of some Whites, could protest their laws openly, and so they passed the *Riotous Assemblies Act 17 of 1956* effectively stopping all protests.

---

[98] Afrikaans for 'White supremacy'.

Between the years of 1951 and 1957, the NP government bulldozed through parliament twelve or more crippling laws that would bring pure misery to any person of colour – the *Bantu Education Act 47 of 1953*, controlling separate education and the *Immorality Act 5 of 1927*, to name but a few. During the latter part of 1958, J G Strijdom passed away and was replaced by Dr H F Verwoerd, who had been a sociology student, specialising in social engineering at Stellenbosch University. He had been a senior minister in Strijdom's cabinet, fulfilling the role of Minister for Black Education. He would become known as the 'Architect of Apartheid!'

The *Promotion of Bantu Self-Government Act 46 of 1959*, which classified Black-owned tribal land into so-called Bantustans,[99] was the one the government savoured. This was grand apartheid at its very best!

In the Northern suburbs of Johannesburg, life went on. Private medical aids were the thing that most people strived to have. Various cricket teams, both provincial and international, visited, but the stage was set, and the United Party was hamstrung; it could do very little to stop the event that was soon to follow.

---

[99] Black homelands.

Chapter 14

It did occur to me that the rule of law had its place in every situation, and in every society! My new friend, the cat, had made this abundantly clear. While she was around, the birds and bugs outside remained completely still.

Since the dawn of time, there have been rules of many kinds and interpretations. The Almighty had, and has, given us, and all of nature, boundaries by which to live. If we are true, and stay within the boundaries, all will go well for us.

But sadly, it is not within our adventurous nature to stay within the confines as set down for us. The result is that we need to employ people to keep us within the laws, as laid down by the authorities. On the surface, there is nothing inherently wrong with this, and every so often, we need to be reminded of where the limitations are, mainly for our own well-being.

But this system of policing, is but a pipe-dream – "Why?" you may ask. Well, it's because the so-called authorities, those who rule us, are not just satisfied with helping us along, they have seen policing as a means to promote their specific ideologies, and to make sure that each of us tows the governing party line.

Instead of rules to protect, rules are made to dominate!

Sarel junior had eventually passed his standard eight school year, after having repeated the year twice! He didn't have anything in mind as far as a career path was concerned. He did know that he didn't want to follow his father and work for the railways. All that grease and the regular hours were certainly not what he had in mind.

One evening, Sarel senior was going through *Die Beeld* newspaper while having his *dop* and he called his son to join him on the porch. "Sarel, my seun,[100] het jy enige idee watter werk jy will doen?"[101]

"*Nee Pa.*[102] Ek weet nie."[103]

"Ek dink jy moet by die Polisie Kollege aantree."[104]

And, so it was that on the first of January 1959, Sarel junior arrived at the local Police College to join the South African Police. At the time, the police were involved in an active recruitment drive, mainly because of the *Police Act 7 of 1958*, which had changed the normal functions of the police to that of maintaining law and order, with special rights to quell unrest. This new Police Act was the brainchild of B J Vorster, the new Minister of Justice in the National parliament of South Africa.

After a six-month, intense training course, Sarel junior qualified as a konstabel,[105] and his whole family gathered in Pretoria to see his passing-out parade. Father Sarel was overcome with joy, and for weeks he embellished the story as he told it to his friends and workmates at the train depot. He concluded every story with, "Nou sal ons die poppe sien dans!"[106]

Sarel junior took up a position at a newly established police

---

[100] Afrikaans for 'my son'.
[101] Afrikaans for 'do you have any idea what work you want to do?'
[102] Afrikaans for 'No, Father'.
[103] Afrikaans for 'I don't know'.
[104] Afrikaans for 'I think you should enrol at the Police College'.
[105] Afrikaans for 'constable'.
[106] Afrikaans for 'Now, things will start happening!'

barracks in Norwood. It was interesting that the government had established a major police barracks in the heart of a quiet suburb like Norwood, but Sarel senior was soon to read about the reason, some evenings later, when he read his newspaper.

It was reported that the voting district, into which Norwood fell, was rapidly becoming a United Party stronghold. Because of the upcoming elections, the government had decided to position Afrikaans-speaking policemen and their families in police barracks, so that when the voting wards were redefined, the vote would go in favour of the National Party.

Maar my mense is slim![107] thought Sarel to himself.

It was just about breakfast time on 21 March 1960 when Sarel junior was busy polishing his boots before going down to the canteen that the order came over the loudspeaker, "Aantree! Aantree!"[108] He grabbed his cap and service revolver and ran down the stairs to the assembly area. When he got there, others were filing into rows.

The officer commanding called them to attention, "Manne! Daar is groot kak[109] in Sharpeville. Klim in die trokke nou!"[110]

Within minutes, eight trucks with about sixty constables and their officers were on their way to Sharpeville, which was south of Johannesburg over the Vaal River, into an area known as the Vaal Triangle. It would take their convoy about two hours to get there. By the time the police reinforcements arrived, it was too late! The dead body count was already at 69, with another 180 injured.

Sarel junior had never seen anything like it before. Dead

---

[107] Afrikaans for 'My people are clever'.
[108] Afrikaans for 'Form up! Form up!'
[109] Afrikaans for 'Men, there is big shit'.
[110] Afrikaans for 'Climb into the trucks now!'

and injured Black people, men, women and even some children were lying scattered in front of the Sharpeville Police Station. Some people were attending to the injured, while policemen guarded the gates to the police station. Sarel noticed a White man with a camera, taking photographs. *Pop! Pop!* went the flash on his camera, and Sarel read a sign on the man's cap that said, "Daily Mail."

Sarel ran up to the policemen standing at the gate, and demanded, "Wat die f... het hier gebeur?"[111]

One of the men answered, "Hulle het hier kom betog oor hulle pasboeke. Ons was so bang! Daar was meer as driehonderd van hulle! Ons moes darem skiet."[112]

The photographs taken by the 'Daily Mail' photographer were seen all over the world, and suddenly the whole of humanity knew the word 'apartheid', and what it meant to carry a passbook. The era of South African prosperity was about to dim! The leader of the nationalist government, Dr H F Verwoerd, with his background in social engineering, would do everything possible to turn the tables on that unfortunate day in Sharpeville.

Sarel senior and Sarel junior would be told, and perhaps persuaded, by the Afrikaans newspapers and radio bulletins that the government, now almost entirely controlled by the Afrikaner Broederbond,[113] a White Afrikaner Calvinist organisation, was in control and that the preserve of government lay in the capable hands of the White minority.

The first thing that Sarel senior spoke about with his

---

[111] Afrikaans for 'What the f... happened here?'
[112] Afrikaans for 'They came to protest about their passbooks, we were so scared! There were more than 300 of them! We just had to shoot'.
[113] Afrikaans for 'Afrikaans brotherhood'.

colleagues was the fact that the ANC and the Pan African Congress (PAC) had been banned. He had also read that the United Nations General Assembly had passed Resolution 1761, condemning apartheid. After all, now that he was sixty, Sarel could claim his railway pension. His daughters were married to confirmed Nationalists, and Sarel junior would get his police salary, no matter what happened.

But there was more to come. The pressure was building on the Union of South Africa; the British government was being compelled by the world to bring her dominion into line. It came sooner than later. In 1960, Sarel and his family, went to the polls, to vote in a White only referendum, with only one question on the ballot paper – 'Should South Africa become a republic?' A simple 'yes' or 'no' was required. By a tiny majority, the White population voted 'yes' and so, on 31 May 1961, The Union of South Africa became the Republic of South Africa.

H F Verwoerd, the architect of apartheid, became the first prime minister! The world held its breath, the economy took a dive and people of colour braced themselves!

Chapter 15

I have often wondered if anyone has ever taken the trouble to do a scientific study on whether bad news or good news travels faster. I am personally of the opinion that bad news travels faster, but I have no scientific statistics to back up my opinion.

Someone succeeds in getting a more profitable position at work; someone receives recognition for their success in their studies; a new baby is born to a household – all these are good news stories! However, there is a saying amongst newspaper editors, and TV presenters, that good news does not sell papers or bring viewers to the screen!

As a result, we are fed daily on the awful things that have happened around us, and we are bombarded with terrifying stories and pictures of men and women doing the most awful things to one another!

These, we are told, are newsworthy stories, and the fact that some medical scientists have discovered a cure for some disease or other rarely finds a place on the front page. Why this is so, I am not sure, but I am convinced that bad news travels faster than good news!

Fundile caught the Putco bus from Edenvale to Soweto. He didn't particularly like the area and had tried to avoid it as much as possible, but Lily had mentioned that a member of her family had found work in the Vaal Triangle. So, he had gone to Soweto to find the Putco bus depot, and the bus that would take him to

Vereeniging in the Vaal Triangle. The bus driver charged him an extra shilling because he had too much luggage. Eventually, the bus pulled out of the depot, and out of Soweto, and made its way onto the Golden Highway, then across the Vaal River to Vereeniging.

Once off the bus, he asked the way to the industrial area, and some helpful folk directed him in the direction of a company called 'Stewarts and Lloyds'. This is where Lily had some family and friends working. By the time Fundile had walked there, it was almost two o'clock, and the main gate to the entrance was locked. Fortunately, after whistling loudly, he was greeted by an out-of-breath man, wearing a neat khaki uniform with a cap that had a shiny silver badge on it. Fundile didn't understand the local language of Sesotho that the man spoke, so he had no option but to speak in isiXhosa. The guard smiled. He was younger than Fundile, so he spoke to him in his home tongue.

In respect, Fundile removed his cap and said that he had come to look for work, and he mentioned the names of Lily's contacts. Again, the guard smiled and opened the heavy metal gates; he helped Fundile carry his luggage through. He then pointed to a sign that read, 'work registration'. After thanking him, Fundile made his way to the registration office. A White official was sitting at a desk. "Yebo," said the man, as Fundile walked into the office and up to the desk.

Fundile removed his cap once more and in his very best English, he said, "Please, boss, I am looking for work."

"How old are you?" The man seemed to be studying a piece of paper on his desk.

"Boss, I have fifty-eight years," came his reply.

"That is very old! Do you have any references?" Still, he

seemed more interested in the paper on his desk!

Fundile took out the references he had in his pocket. One was the original certificate from the nuns, which was now quite tattered and torn, and a much newer one, typed and signed by the MacDonalds. The official eventually looked up, folded the piece of paper he had been reading and took the papers from Fundile.

Fundile reckoned that the man was about the same age as his son. He opened each document, starting with his school certificate and ending with the one from the MacDonalds. He put all these in front of him on the desk, and said, "I see you worked as a gardener. We make pipes here. We do not do gardening! I cannot help you!"

"Sorry, boss. I also worked on the mines in Johannesburg, for thirty years, and I was a shift leader."

"Why didn't you say that before?" He now looked at Fundile with a bit more interest. "Where is your paper from the mines?"

Fundile was stumped! "Sorry boss," he said shaking his head. "*Eh*, sorry, boss!"

"Yes, what are you trying to say?" demanded the now irritable younger man.

"Sorry, boss. The boss at the mine didn't give me a paper." He tried his best to explain.

"How can I believe you, that you worked on the mines?" he asked in a doubting tone.

"No, boss. I am speaking the truth. Please, my boss, it is true!"

"Wait here!" the official instructed, and he rose from his chair and went into an adjoining office. He returned about five or so minutes later. Fundile was still standing with his cap in his hands. "You are madala,[114] but I can give you 'sebenza'[115] in the factory. Come tomorrow. Do you have a pass?"

"Yebo, my boss! Thank you, my boss! I will come tomorrow, my boss!" and Fundile walked backwards to the door, bowing as he spoke. He left his luggage with the guard at the gate, who was delighted that Fundile had found work. He asked the guard for clear instructions on how to get to Sharpeville, the local township nearby, originally established by the founder of Stewarts and Lloyds, some years before. The guard told him the shortest route and explained where he might find shared lodgings.

*

It was in December of that same year that Khazimela turned twenty-four years old, and obtained his bachelor's degree from the University of Fort Hare, majoring in political science and human resources. The entire Khumalo family were very excited. Sadly, Fundile couldn't join in the celebration, as he had not yet earned enough leave. But Langalethu, the second son, had organised the slaughter of a young bull, and Asiphesona and Bonga, his daughters, helped Iviwe with the food for the celebration.

The day was a huge success! Khazimela was the first in his entire village, let alone in the family, to qualify from university. The family wrote to Fundile, and explained the day in detail; Fundile was delighted! Even though the employment he had was that of a factory sweeper, he was just grateful to have some work!

---

[114] IsiXhosa word for 'old'.
[115] IsiXhosa word for 'work'.

After the celebrations had passed and the new year began, Iviwe could see that Khazimela was getting restless at the family kraal. Not long after, he spoke to his mother about going to a place where he could utilise his degree and make some money. He soon packed his belongings and left for the city of East London, a major port on the east coast of the Union of South Africa. He left with the promise that he would send home some money as soon as he found work.

But he soon discovered after he had found lodgings in the adjoining Black township of Mdantsane that although he had a degree, this gave him little, or no, scope in finding work in the commercial field in East London. Soon, he became very frustrated, and in the evenings, the talk in the township always turned to the pass laws; how many people had been arrested for not complying, and now the talk was turning to how the White government was starting even greater racial segregation by establishing, what were called *Bantustans*. This would put the Xhosa into the Ciskei Homeland, the Zulus into Zululand, and so on, with the other Black groups.

The talk was becoming more disturbing every day! Of course, this was exactly what Khazimela's professors at Fort Hare had spoken about at length. Everything about this, in the way the Blacks were being ignored, made Khazimela's blood boil and kept him awake at night.

A week later, Khazimela knocked on the door of the registered office of the Eastern province brand of the ANC and handed his credentials to the local secretary general. He was welcomed into their midst and immediately signed up. They issued him with booklets and papers to read, and all the encouragement he needed to recruit other interested parties.

Khazimela soon learnt, from his landlord that the ANC did not pay the rent or for his food, and it was time for him to now get a paying job. He was indeed lucky! Round about the time of his graduation, the government had passed the *Bantu Education Act 47 of 1953*, meaning there was racially separate education, for Blacks.

Thanks to the local Native Affairs Department, in East London, and with a view to the possible establishment of Independent Black States, a building had been earmarked for Black children to go to school. There was a massive shortage of Black teachers, so, when Khazimela laid his qualification on the desk of the recruiting officer, he was immediately hired. His qualifying subjects were of little or no importance.

Soon, Khazimela was earning a good salary and could afford to discuss policies at the ANC office, at the weekends.

*

Fundile rose early, on the morning of 21 March in 1960, and he dressed, then had a cup of sweet tea and a slice of bread and jam. He took his cap, padlocked the door to his room and started making his way to the Putco bus stop. He had walked this path and passed the Sharpeville police station for the past year or so. But this morning, be noticed a crowd of people moving in the direction of the police station. He couldn't quite hear what they were chanting, and some were even shouting something about a *dompas*. As they drew nearer the police station, Fundile could see that they were waving their passbooks in the air.

Automatically, he felt in his back pocket for his own pass and, satisfied that it was there, he walked on. Suddenly, all hell broke loose, and he could hear gunfire coming from the police station. He was not yet at the police station, but he could hear screaming and wailing, and the crowd were no longer ahead of him, they had turned and were running towards him – about two hundred and fifty people! Still, gunfire could be heard and the screaming, but this time the wailing went on much longer.

Men and women, and even some children, ran past him, shouting, "Run!"

Still, people ran and still, the firing continued. The pain of a bullet slammed into Fundile's shoulder, knocking him to the ground, and the people continued to run. And then, it was over. Silence, just silence, and blue smoke hung over the area. The smell of cordite filled the air, and Fundile managed to get up onto one knee. His shoulder ached, and his right arm hung limp at his side. But he was alive! However, within his range of sight, he could see many motionless bodies. Others, like him, were injured but alive, and in the forefront, standing in line, were the policemen of the Sharpeville Constabulary.

News of the shooting spread from Sharpeville, across the world, within hours. The township itself was reeling with trauma, concern and above all, hate! This hate soon filtered into all the offices of the ANC and the PAC and people, like Khazimela, who had a vested interest in the whole affair, did not take the matter lightly. The seams of displeasure, suspicion and hatred were beginning to take root.

It was no surprise to Khazimela to hear that his father had lost the use of his arm because of the shooting, and could no longer work; he had finally been sent home.

Equally, when the Whites held a referendum in 1961 to decide whether the Union should become a Republic, Khazimela and his comrades knew that it was only a matter of days before the ANC would be outlawed. It didn't take long, or even much thought, for Khazimela to decide to join *uMkhonto we Sizwe*[116] and form an underground cell.

---

[116] IsiXhosa for 'Shield of the Nation'.

Chapter 16

I felt a tear come to my eye, and the bitter taste of defeat, or anger, I am not sure which, welled up in my throat. I swallowed hard, and without thinking reached out my hand and stroked the cat next to me, asleep and oblivious to my situation.

I rose from my position on the pew, and as I did, I subconsciously looked at my watch. It was just about noon, and this time triggered my senses, telling me that I was hungry and a little thirsty. I have no idea why I did it, but I walked down the aisle to the back of the place of worship, and there I found a drinking glass on the shelf, which I filled with water from the cold tap in the basin.

I drained the glass quickly as if I had never had water before, and then I refilled it and sipped it a little slower. Grateful for the drink, I rinsed the glass and replaced it on the shelf. No one would even know that I had used it!

Thankful for the refreshment, I returned to my seat, and to the sleeping cat who hadn't stirred! The tear in my eye had gone, but I was still angry. How could my country ever sort itself out? How would each group accommodate the other? How long would we have to live on a knife edge?

The English newspapers, *The Star* and *The Sunday Times*, carried the story of the Sharpeville tragedy for days. The JSE took a real pounding, and the FTSE All Share Index dropped dramatically. The British government also took a hammering.

After all, the Union of South Africa was still one of its dominions. World-renowned brands considered their position in the country and its economy.

At the Porter-Smith home, Peter Henry, the eldest son, completed his compulsory three months of army training and was technically on standby. When Sharpeville burst onto the scene, the National Party government thought it wise to put certain citizen force regiments on standby. Peter Henry's regiment was one such unit. For days he had to be ready to move at any given time in case there was a backlash to the events the previous week.

But nothing happened, other than the establishment of various boards of enquiry, who studied the events of that 21st day in March 1960. South Africa became the pariah of the world. The word '*apartheid*' became the buzz word in overseas newspaper articles, and the National Party government was left with no option but to send attaches and government representatives to London, to seek independence from the British Empire.

So, on 5 October 1960, six months after Sharpeville, a referendum was held, and the White electorate was asked to vote, either 'yes' or 'no' to independence. By a slim majority of 52% to 47%, the electorate voted in favour of leaving the Commonwealth and forming the Republic of South Africa. The Province of Natal, on the east coast, was the only province to vote against leaving. The Union of South Africa, and its apartheid policies, were such an embarrassment to the British government that it didn't take much persuading to allow South Africa to break ties.

On 31 May 1961, Charles (Blackie) Swart ceased to be the Governor of the Union of South Africa, and instead, became the first State President. This was in name only as all the powers of the new Republic rested in the hands of the National Party government, led by that architect of apartheid, Dr H F Verwoerd. The country was now on its own, and it was up to the people of South Africa to make the best of a particularly bad situation.

In the northern suburbs of Johannesburg, the Porter-Smiths were faced with a bit of a dilemma. Their second son, David, had finished primary school and was due to go to a private high school, as his brother had done some years before, but there was a problem. Finances did not permit, so he was sent to a government high school, with the promise that he would go to university thereafter.

In the meantime, with the advent of the Republic of South Africa, a whole vestiture of symbols had to change. The currency changed from British pounds, shillings and pence, to decimal rands and cents. The old imperialistic form of weights and measures also had to change to the decimal system. And so, the government set about teaching the entire population how to pay, measure and weigh in the decimal system. Some inventive person coined the phrase 'Decimal Dan' (the one-cent man). For the next year or so, the entire population, both Black and White, had to learn this new monetary and measurement decimal system.

Children at school had to unlearn the Imperial system and learn the decimal system instead. In time, it all worked out, but the rand, British pound and US dollar exchange rate started to wobble in financial circles. With all the hype of the New Republic and the decimal system, the newspapers, read mainly in the northern suburbs, scarcely covered the banning of the ANC and the fact that Nelson Mandela, and twenty-seven others, had been acquitted of high treason.

There was even less about Mandela and his comrades going underground in March 1961 to have military training outside the country, and starting up the military wing, known as *uMkhonto we sizwe*. It seemed it wasn't that important.

But all that was about to change! Michael John and Betye, and a group of their friends, were having a braai at their Orchards home when the men started discussing the fact that Mandela had been captured at a place called Howick, in the Province of Natal.

"Who is this Mandela?" asked Tim, one of the guests standing at the fire, watching the lamb chops sizzle.

"Who knows! Who cares!" came from another guest, Martin.

But it did matter! Over the next two years, the Rivonia trial, concerning various cases of sabotage, would be the newspaper headlines and stories each day. The result of the trial was that each of those on trial were sentenced to life imprisonment. And they were whisked away to serve their sentences on Robben Island.[117]

David's years at high school were generally uneventful, except for the fact that all school reference books, especially those of history, were rewritten to give a distinct bias to the Afrikaner, and the conquering and submission of the Black tribes of Southern Africa. An emphasis was placed on the Afrikaaner volk[118] and how they had subdued the Black people, and indeed the English-speaking colonists. In fact, very little was taught about the British winning the two Boer wars. The National Anthem was written in Afrikaans.

---

[117] An island off the coast of Cape Town.
[118] Afrikaans for 'people' or 'population'.

The rivalry between English and Afrikaans-speaking high schools was tangible. Better equipped and with better facilities were all part of the government-run education department's plan to upgrade Afrikaans schools. Afrikaans–English apartheid was beginning to rear its ugly head.

There was much excitement in the years 1965 and 1966. The fictional character, James Bond, made his debut on the bookshelves of good booksellers, and onto the silver screen. The Beatles – John, Paul, George, and Ringo – were slowly, but surely, making their mark on the hit parade of Springbok and LM commercial radio stations.

March 1966 saw a general election, for Whites only, to return H F Verwoerd to power. As was common practice, and had been for quite a few years, The Rand Easter Show was held in the area known as Milner Park, just west of the University of the Witwatersrand, over the Easter period. Thousands of people flocked to the show over the two-week period.

On a particular show day, 9 April 1966, a special guest was due to visit the show. This guest was the Prime Minister of the Republic, Dr H F Verwoerd. His motor cavalcade stopped, and as he exited the car, two shots were fired, both hitting Verwoerd in the face. The shooter was a certain David Pratt. Miraculously, Verwoerd was only injured and lived to pass many draconian acts of apartheid law.

However, in September of the same year, a deranged cleaner, Demetrius Tsafendas, got close enough, inside the Houses of Parliament, to assassinate Verwoerd by inflicting various stab wounds. The National Party government was rocked to its core, while the rest of South Africa sighed with relief. Days later, B J Vorster, the Minister of Justice, came to power, and South Africa waited to see if apartheid would at last show signs of weakness. But it didn't!

Meanwhile, in the Porter-Smith household, the end of the year was rapidly approaching, and David would be writing his matriculation examinations intending to go to university the following year. But fate played a nasty hand, and in the October of that year, he received his call-up papers for compulsory military training.

At that time, all the boys in his matric class had to go to their nearest police station and register for the ballot system. Each of the eighty boys in that class waited to see whether their name would be selected for the ballot system. Most of the boys came from middle-class families, and the great majority, or their parents, were anti-government, and anti-any system.

Out of the eighty boys that signed up, only two were actually 'balloted' and David was one of them!

At the end of 1966, the matriculation results were posted, and more than 50% of the class left the country for other lands and opportunities.

The army training was to last for nine months, and so in April 1967, David found himself at the Artillery School, in the army barracks in Potchefstroom (a major military base, some kilometres away to the west of Johannesburg). About thirty untrained soldiers were assigned to each barracks, and in David's barracks, he was the only English-speaking person. All instructions and lectures were in Afrikaans. Oddly enough, all the training manuals were in English! That is because they were printed while South Africa had still been a British dominion.

The instructors, all Afrikaans-speaking, obviously taught in that language, and it became very apparent that David would rapidly have to learn to understand and speak the language. He had learnt Afrikaans at school, up to matric, but in the suburbs where he lived and moved around, there was no need for the language, and most of them didn't speak Afrikaans unless absolutely necessary.

Here in the army, however, it was going to be different, and he would have to speak Afrikaans, or sink. He soon learnt that only three out of the whole intake had achieved a matriculation certificate, with the rest of the 'boys' having only a standard eight (a school passing out certificate) and many of them wanted to learn how to speak English. So, instead of engaging David in Afrikaans, in the evenings, they would insist that David converse with them in English.

"A very strange set of circumstances," remarked David to his father, on the family's first visit to see him.

As the days passed into weeks and months, so came the time for promotions. Many of the Afrikaans boys received promotions, but the English-speaking boys, with matriculation certificates and the highest army examination rates, could not be ignored, and so David also gained promotion. It was at one of these ceremonies that David made a deal with himself. He would make a point of being just that bit better than them, and obtain the rank so that he wouldn't have to be told how to conduct himself.

The initial army training came to an end, and David now had to face three lots of three-week camps, to be completed over the next three years. David returned to Johannesburg, and because funds didn't permit him to go to university, he was now firmly in the job market.

Fortune smiled quite quickly upon him, and after completing a university-sponsored aptitude test, the results revealed, and recommended, that he consider approaching the South African Broadcasting Company for a position in radio. Of course, at that time, South African television was only a dream because the Calvinistic fathers deemed television too worldly for the South African public.

David, thus, started at the SABC early in 1968 and was placed in the presentation department, working firstly for the 'A' station (the English station), but he also worked for the 'B' station (the Afrikaans station). Those working in the presentation department were predominantly Afrikaans-speaking. This was obviously so because the SABC was the mouthpiece of the apartheid government.

The same criteria that applied in the Defence Force, applied at the broadcasting company as well, in that the Afrikaans-speaking colleagues were given the promotions and awards. The only way to get anywhere was to be better qualified so that you couldn't be ignored. This worked to a point!

Chapter 17

Isn't it funny how one's mind can change so easily, and mine on that day was no different! I have no idea why, but I suddenly found myself thinking of the changing of the guards at Buckingham Palace! So smart and orderly they are! Such precision, such pride and grandeur! The changing of the guard has happened so many times; so many new ranks every year, yet the same drill and the same spectacle!

I shook my head, trying to get back to my original thoughts, and in so doing, I woke the cat, who promptly decided to leave me, and disappeared out of the window, as quickly as it had climbed in.

Clearly, my visit was not going to be the same. The old, in this case, the cat, had gone, and I had no idea what would fill its place.

I particularly listened to hear the birds and bugs again, but there was nothing. Just the heat of the noon-day sun could be felt, and the cool breeze through the window was also gone!

Sarel senior had just gone on pension at the age of sixty, and under the rules and regulations of the railways, he would get about one-third of his final salary, each month as a pension for the rest of his life. The National Party government were good to their employees, and so Sarel could at last relax.

Sarel junior had left home and was in the police barracks in Norwood. It was now only Sarel senior, Petronella, their second son, Fanus, and daughters Mimi and Anna, staying in the subsidised house in Roodepoort. Even though Sarel had retired, the family realised that money was tight. Fanus would follow in his father's footsteps, and get an apprenticeship with the railways the following year. Mimi, who was nineteen, was working as a clerk at the post office, where she had been for the past three years.

Eighteen-year-old Anna had fallen pregnant and would have to look for work. She wasn't sure who the baby's father was, and her father had promised to bliksem[119] the young man if he got hold of him! To make ends meet, Sarel had bought a second-hand welding machine and had converted the backyard into a workshop, where he would take on welding jobs. "Security gates and doors," he explained to the neighbour.

Sadly, later that year, Petronella died. The family had taken her to the J G Strijdom Hospital, not far from their home, where she succumbed to her illness. Everyone was devastated, but fortunately, her two-month stay in the hospital had cost them very little, as it was a state hospital, and the stay was subsidised by their health plan.

Mimi stepped straight into her mother's shoes, cooking and cleaning for the family. This gave Sarel extra time to read the newspaper, and to privately cheer on the government with the new barbaric laws they put in place. Sarel's *dop* was still relatively cheap, and Mimi always made sure that there was a cold Coca-Cola in the fridge for her father to mix with his drink at night.

Sarel junior was a good policeman, and his talents were soon noticed. The family were delighted when he phoned to say that he had received a promotion, but that he was being

---

[119] Afrikaans for 'hurt'.

transferred to the Special Task Unit, responsible for assisting South West African and Rhodesian police forces, particularly the 'bush wars', as he explained to his father. He wasn't sure how long he would be away but promised to telephone when he returned.

Sarel did return in November 1965, just for his 'annual leave' ,he told his family, but that he would have to urgently return to Rhodesia to assist with things there, especially as the prime minister, Ian Smith, had earlier that month announced a Unilateral Declaration of Independence (UDI). The world shook its fist at Rhodesia and called Smith a rogue. The United Nations passed various declarations, condemning this sort of politics, and South Africa sent food, arms and ammunition, petrol and aid to assist the newly declared independent government.

While on leave from the 'bush war', Sarel junior took the opportunity to marry his long-time sweetheart, Elizabeth, who worked as a nurse at the Johannesburg General Hospital (Joburg Gen). The family all pitched in to make the wedding a happy one, and friends helped with the catering for the reception held at the local Scout Hall. Sarel and Elizabeth went to Margate, on the south coast of Natal, for their honeymoon.

But soon it was back to duty for Sarel. Fortunately, Elizabeth was able to keep her bedroom at the nurses' home at the hospital, for a few months at least. Sarel junior was back, sooner than everyone expected, as the unit had been recalled to deal with local civil unrest. His section was in the thick of things, and they had been put on stand-by at the Rand Show, on the day that there was an attempt on Verwoerd's life. Shortly after the prime minister's recovery, the government worried about another possible attempt when Verwoerd was to make a speech at the Voortrekker[120] Monument in Pretoria. The speech was about the rights of Whites in civilisation in Africa.

Although the National Party secured a landslide victory in the poll, 126/80, the more moderate section of the Afrikaans population felt that the government, under Verwoerd, was not doing much for the Blacks but was, also, not doing enough for the White farmers. Added to this, the verligtes[121] were anti-Bantustans – the separate homelands for the Blacks.

Sarel explained to Elizabeth that Verwoerd was a target from many points of view. So, he was not surprised to learn from his superiors, later that year, that Verwoerd had been assassinated in Cape Town. That city was a long way from Johannesburg, so Sarel and his unit were not affected. One month later, Elizabeth told her husband, that he was to become a father.

Sarel was at the top of his game over the next three years. The *Terrorism Act 83 of 1967* was passed by Parliament. This was due to acts of sabotage and terrorism activities by the armed wing of the ANC – *uMkhonto we Sizwe*, in South Africa, and the building up of ZAPU in the armed struggle in Rhodesia. The daily and national newspapers were filled with articles on the suppression and acts of terrorism, and the courts were filled with bleak judgements. B J Vorster had tightened the grip on apartheid, but at last, some good news!

Elizabeth saw the article on the front page of the newspaper and she brought it to Sarel's attention. Dr Christiaan Barnard, a heart specialist at the Groote Schuur Hospital in Cape Town, had successfully transplanted a heart into an elderly man, suffering from incurable heart disease. At last, the world's view

---

[120] Afrikaans for 'Pioneer'.
[121] Afrikaans for 'moderate wing'.

of South Africa changed for the positive. On the southern tip of Africa, a South African surgeon, had turned the world of medical science upside down! There was hope, and just for a while, the political focus was not on the negative parts of South Africa.

But the euphoria didn't last long. Soon the new State President of the Republic of South Africa, J J Fouche, was inaugurated in 1968 to become the second man in this position in the history of the republic, and the government was obliged to now enforce the *Internal Security Act (Suppression of Communism Act) 44 of 1950*, and thus this act was later amended in 1968.

It wasn't long after this that Sarel was sent off to the border between South Africa and Botswana because Azanian People's Liberation Army (APLA) were trying to infiltrate their members into South Africa from Botswana in the west and Mozambique to the east. He missed the birth of his son, Jan, while he was up on the border. He was delighted to receive the news from his Commanding Officer, upon it being relayed on the bush telephone. This did mean that he, Elizabeth, and the baby would have to find a bigger place to live when he returned home.

The banned ANC in South Africa, through their exiles in Africa, held their first conference in Tanzania. This received much press coverage, and by the time Sarel returned home, the United Nations were well under way in obtaining support for the isolation of South Africa because of its apartheid policies. There was even talk about sanctions and a possible arms embargo.

Sarel and his family found a new home. Sarel senior helped

the young couple scrape together a small deposit, and the local building society was quick to grant them a bond, at a good rate because Sarel would be paying monthly via his police housing allowance. Their new home was in Alberton, a medium-sized town, southeast of Johannesburg.

In Natal, to the extreme east of the country, one of the first Black homelands would see the inauguration of its first CEO – Chief Mangosuthu Buthelezi. The event received much publicity, and Sarel watched with interest. The year 1971 came and went with various oppressive laws being passed, and the world cried foul but did little about it.

The following year brought news that did affect Sarel junior. The majority of the world, through the offices of the United Nations, placed an arms embargo on South Africa. However, suppliers of arms could not agree on the terms, and while some weaponry became scarce, the police force soon found other willing suppliers worldwide.

When Elizabeth got home from her day shift as a newly appointed theatre nurse at the hospital near their home, she explained to Sarel that a Chinese colleague had announced that the Chinese people in South Africa had been given 'White' status in the country. She went on to tell him that she was pregnant. He was delighted.

The arms embargo fizzled, but the Arab States and the African oil producers announced that they were placing an oil embargo on South Africa. The country sat up and took notice! Sasol, the South African oil company, had been established in 1955 because of the coal reserves in the country, from which petroleum could be sourced. The process of converting coal into petroleum was clever and secretly guarded, but it was expensive. So, Sasol had been running for many years at a commercial loss, but it was a strategic asset. So, when the oil embargo was mooted, much commercial activity was focused on Sasol's plant in Secunda, just 118 kilometres from Johannesburg.

Sarel junior took an interest in this because his younger brother, Fanus, had recently moved to Secunda to join the Sasol operation, which had become financially much more viable due to rising fuel prices. The result of this embargo, and the building of Sasol, drew attention away from the banning of the activist, Steve Biko, and the leadership of the United Party being taken over by Harry Schwartz.

However, the peace was soon broken when a 100,000-strong strike broke out in Durban, Natal. Sarel and his Special Task team were sent to sort out possible threats to the province and the government. Fortunately, the strike was not violent, but it marked a turning point in labour relations. The strike was not organised by the more established labour unions but by ordinary people wanting better conditions in the work place.

Still, apartheid carried on, and people were suppressed. Segregation was the order of the day, and dissimilar budgets were spent on education and social upliftment. The homeland policies were succeeding in some areas, while in others, the opposition was the order of the day. When 1974 dawned, it was not surprising that the general elections would be a little different. And they were! The New Zealand government had placed a ban on all sports events with South Africa. This was a setback for the country which was pro-rugby and cricket.

Portugal had just come through a coup and had given up control of its colonies in Africa, including Angola and Mozambique. Pik Botha, the new Minister of Foreign Affairs, had been instructed to start engaging with the United Nations on the reforms that South Africa was contemplating.

The result of the general election was interesting, and a matter of discussion at Sarel junior's dinner table. The outcome of the vote revealed 57% to the National Party, 32% to the United Party, 5.3% to the new Progressive Party, and alarmingly, 3.6% to the extreme right-wing party, the HNP. Sarel concluded the discussion by saying, "Maar, ons het darem gewen!"[122] The NP government did take note, and Nico Diedericks became the newest state president. Of the original proposed Homelands, there were in total, ten which were created in South Africa at the time. There were Transkei; Boputhatswana; Ciskei; Venda; Gazankulu; KaNgwane; KwaNdebele; KwaZulu; Lebowa and QwaQwa. A bill was passed giving Black children free education with the proviso that half of the instruction be done in the Afrikaans language.

Alarmingly, for Sarel and the South African Defence Force (SADF), Angola to the north of South West Africa had become independent and had employed Cuban forces to assist in propping up the new government. The world hardly took notice, when the SADF engaged the Angolan–Cuban forces at the first battle of Ebo. Even less was said about the South African Navy embarking on a rescue mission into Luanda, to fetch members of the SADF after the battle of Ebo. The world had not taken notice of Frelimo taking over in Mozambique the year before, either.

By 1976, Sarel had reached the rank of Captain, in the police unit, and he had just over one hundred men, mainly White, under his command. Part of this group were 'informers',[123] who moved amongst the population, gathering

---

[122] Afrikaans for 'But at least we won!'
[123] Plain clothes operatives.

information to pass onto their superiors about happenings on the ground. One such happening came to Sarel's attention when the informers reported that the youth, children of school-going age, in Soweto were unhappy about learning in Afrikaans. He passed this information on to the top brass, but he told Elizabeth, "Niemand het geluister!"[124]

On 16 June 1976, the youth of Soweto rioted. Between ten and twenty thousand of them gathered at the Orlando Stadium. They flooded the streets with children; they burnt cars and buildings and destroyed vehicles. The police over-reacted, using live ammunition. Tear-gas was thrown into the crowd, and arrests were made. News of the rioting children soon spread to the adjoining township. As night fell, the unlit townships became even more terrifying, blinded by the dark, the police fired into the blackness. The students looted liquor stores, and wandered around shouting, "Amandla!"[125]

In the morning, the official death toll was 23, as claimed by the government. But the number of people who died is usually given as 176, with other estimates up to 700. The number of wounded was over a thousand. Most victims were under 23 years of age, and by the end of that year, 575 people had died, not all at the hands of the police. About six thousand were arrested.

The outcome was that schools could choose their medium of instruction. Some changes came, whereby Blacks could now operate their own businesses, and doctors and lawyers could practice in the townships. These were positive, but the sting in the tail was that police could detain people without a trial. The result was the detention of hundreds of people.

---

[124] Afrikaans for 'no one listened'.
[125] IsiXhosa word for 'Power!'

Thousands of young people left the country, disillusioned with the government's crack-down and harassment by the police. Many didn't finish their education and chose to go into military camps in Africa, where they received anti-government training. The stage had been set!

Chapter 18

What can a person do, I thought to myself, when that person has reached an absolute dead end, and exhausted every other option?

I stared up at the main wall in front of me and noticed a small, yet determined gecko, trying to catch a fly that was about a metre away from it. Here was the gecko's lunch, but each time he moved closer to his prey, it would move to another position.

I again reprimanded myself for allowing my concentration to wane. What do people do when they are as frustrated as a gecko?

The answer was obvious, but I didn't like the answer. They go into fighting mode! They lose all their sense of value, save for their cause, and fight, man to man. Yes! That's what they do! I said to myself. Rules go out the door; feelings flare into uncontrollable passions and reasonable people die in the process!

Just then, the gecko got close enough, and in an instant the fly was in its mouth, wings flapping, but to no avail. It was just a matter of time before it would be lunch!

The ANC and the PAC were, without a doubt, permanently banned, sending hundreds into exile, particularly to the military bases in Africa. Kazimela made his way to a house in Soweto one night, where he had been sent by his comrades in the Johannesburg cell. He was told to only take a small bag with him, with clothes and enough food and water for about three days. He did not have to worry about extra clothes or shoes, because once he reached his destination, he would be supplied with everything he needed.

Kazimela had no idea where he was going, other than it was out of the country. He knocked on the door of the Soweto house. It was poorly lit, with the only real light coming from a flood light high up on a mast, further down the road. A mongrel barked from the yard of the house across the road, but other than that, nobody took any notice of him.

The door opened. Behind the door were two men. It was Sipho who asked what he wanted, and the other man said nothing, except look Kazimela up and down. "Ndingu[126] Khazimela Khumalo."

"Yima,"[127] said Sipho, and left him standing at the door, under the observation of the other man. After about five minutes Sipho returned and instructed him to come in. The three men now walked down a passage to a bigger room, where there was a table and a single upright-chair, with other more comfortable chairs, where men already sat waiting.

"Hlala,"[128] said one of the men, and Khazimela sat on the hard, single one at the table. The interrogation began, and he answered all the questions with ease. They were impressed that he had a university degree, but the questions soon turned to his political views, especially those on separate development and apartheid. They particularly liked the fact that he hated the White police because they had shot his father at Sharpeville.

He obviously passed the interrogation, and at about five

---

[126] IsiXhosa for 'I am'.
[127] IsiXhosa for 'Wait'.
[128] IsiXhosa for 'Sit'.

o'clock the next morning, a van arrived at the house. Khazimela and another man, Sandile, got into the back of the vehicle with their luggage and their signed passbooks. The door closed, and the van drove off on its way to Botswana. The van avoided the official border post between South Africa and Botswana; instead, it made its way on a track leading to a house in Lobatse. The van stopped, and the two men were told to get out.

"We will rest here, and then drive again tonight," announced the driver. "Welcome to Botswana." The three men sat under a tree in the courtyard of the 'safe' house, and Khazimela counted at least six people who were busy inside the house. "Well gentlemen," said the driver. "This is the first part of a long journey for you."

When Sandile spoke, the man answered. "Sorry, I don't speak isiXhosa. I am from Botswana, and we speak English here. Where we are going, you will have to speak English because the people you will meet speak very little English and, definitely, no isiXhosa!"

Khazimela and Sandile nodded. The driver continued, "It's best that you say nothing, and talk very little. It is not safe here. Botswana is in the middle of three White controlled countries. South Africa in the south; Southern Rhodesia in the south east, and South West Africa to the west. We are not even sure about our northern neighbour, Angola. My country cannot afford to make any of her neighbours angry or suspicious, so just say very little. Rest a bit now. We will move again tonight. The driver moved off into the house, and the two men ate the lunches they had brought with them.

The trip to Serowe, further north, was uneventful, and it took most of the night. But the next day, the driver allowed the two men to sit in the cab with him. At about noon, they reached the border between Botswana and Southern Rhodesia, an area known as the Caprivi Strip. At this point, the driver handed his passengers over to the skipper of the *Freedom Ferry*, which crossed the Zambezi River directly into Zambia. This route was known to the exiles that were fleeing to Tanzania as the 'Pipeline'.

Khazimela was surprised at the proficiency of the pipeline, and all those involved, for it took him and Sandile just over a week to get to the training camp site, Kongawa in the hinterland of Tanzania. Their training started the very next day and included weapon handling, map reading, bomb planting, and of course military discipline, along with much ANC doctrine.

The Kongawa camp was full to capacity with *Umkhonto we Sizwe* recruits, all these because of their hate for the apartheid system and their oppression back home. Camp conditions were basic in the extreme, and there were already grumblings about the food and accommodation, but the main discord was boredom and the lack of future operations and targets. After all, these recruits had come to see action. And unfortunately, there seemed to be very little, except for the marching up and down parade fields, and the stripping and assembling of AK47 rifles!

News soon arrived at the camp that the ANC would hold their first conference in Tanzania, and there was talk that action would come fast and furious thereafter. Particularly, because APLA had tried to infiltrate South Africa, via Botswana and Mozambique.

Outside broadcasts confirmed that the United Nations had passed another resolution, supporting the isolation of South Africa because of apartheid. Back home, Mangosuthu Buthelelzi had been appointed CEO of the Black homeland of KwaZulu. At about this time, the Tanzanian government was no longer prepared to host the ANC recruits because of disputes within the hierarchy of the party, and the whole camp was relocated to Morogoro in Zambia.

This move gave respite to the boredom of the recruits at the camp, and they were particularly pleased that the new camp was closer to the South African border, and a springboard for sabotage attacks. The camp did move, and the next five-and-a-half years were again boring, once the euphoria of the new base had worn off.

There was a lighter moment when the camp heard of the new arms embargo against South Africa. Those who had Chinese friends were surprised to hear that they had been given White status by the NP government. This further enraged the recruits. Then they heard that Steve Biko, the activist, had been banned and that African and Arab states had placed an oil embargo as well.

But in 1974, yet another general election was held, and the National Party won the poll. The talk in the camp was about the far-right wing, the HNP, doing better than expected. This was not well received by those in the camp, in Zambia. On a brighter note, the new foreign minister was suggesting some reforms at the United Nations Assembly, even though New Zealand had banned all sports with the Republic.

In the first quarter of 1974, the Portuguese government had been dissolved, and news reached the recruits that the people were withdrawing from their colonies, namely in Angola and Mozambique. This news was celebrated in the camp. At last, the White Portuguese colonialists would be leaving, and handing their countries over to their rightful owners. But the uproar would not last long. During the next year, the freedom fighters, Frelimo, would be at war in Mozambique, and in

Angola, the first Cuban combat troops would arrive.

Khazimela and Sandile were not sure what to believe. At home, Blacks were to receive free education, and the original homelands were to be consolidated into just thirty-four. Still, terrible boredom and a feeling of false expectation filled their hearts. Khazimela longed for home.

He didn't have to wait long because, on 16 June 1976, all hell broke loose in Soweto and the surrounding townships. School children had been killed by the apartheid government. This news was told to them at the midday briefing at Morogoro. Was this the spark that was needed to get the recruits out of the camp and back into South Africa, to start the onslaught on the South African government? Tempers ran high in the camp, among the *uMkhonto we Sizwe* recruits. The propagandists went into overdrive, and once again training was started in earnest. It was only in 1978 that Khazimela, Sandile, and others got their first assignment. B J Vorster had become the new State President, and P W Botha took over the role of Prime Minister.

Khazimela, Sandile, and six others left the camp at Morogoro and made their way back into the Republic via Botswana. The journey was difficult and dangerous, as they were carrying some arms with them. One slip at the border post would mean instant arrest. Once back in South Africa, they made their way to Soweto and various safe houses. They had to mingle with the crowd, and of course, wear normal clothes. Instructions were given at the safe houses, always at night behind locked doors, for fear of police informants and government spies.

The cell to which Khazimela belonged, was given four targets – three local ones, and one in Port Elizabeth. They received the one in Port Elizabeth because Khazimela had mentioned that he knew the area well. The first target was the Daveyton Police Station, so on 2 February, the cell attacked the police station. Shots were fired, but no one was hurt. The attack received much publicity, which was the modus operandi. The attack was a success!

The cell then moved to an unspecified target location in Johannesburg itself. The home-made bomb was found by the police, and disarmed. Not much in the way of publicity, but enough news to stir the readers.

And, so, on to Port Elizabeth. This was more difficult, and transport plans for the six *Umkhonto we Sizwe* cadres had to be meticulously planned. Various people, sympathetic to the cause, were called on, and eventually, two cars made their way to the offices of Bantu Affairs, right in the heart of the city. Khazimela was in charge of this target, and he directed operations well. It was mid-March, and the bomb device was planted against the main wall of the office block. There was a huge blast, and some structural damage, but no casualties! But the success was newsworthy and was recorded in all the newspapers in the country and overseas.

Back in Soweto, in December, the group successfully detonated another bomb. This time, at the Soweto Council Offices. This too had the desired hallmark of a terrorist attack and was now drawing attention from the government.

The next year was a basket of mixed successes and failures, and Khazimela's cell was put on high alert after it was learnt that another cell had been identified in a northern town called Zeerust, and they had to flee to Botswana. None the less, bombs were placed, and exploded, at Canada Railway station, and the Moroka Police Station, where a policeman was killed, as well as one at Orlando Police Station.

Unfortunately for the cell, the police found two arms caches, one at Fort Beaufort and one at King Williamstown; a bomb was found and disarmed on a Soweto bus, and another in a town called Alice. These failures were recorded in the newspapers and on radio and TV stations. This was all part of the guerrilla tactics.

The year had generally been a success for Khazimela and Sandile, but it was dampened by the news that the SADF had attacked, and destroyed, an ANC base at Nova Caterque, a training centre the two men knew well! The attack reinforced their resolve, all the more, and bigger and more pronounced targets were set for the new year, starting with a daylight attack on the Silverton bank, just east of Pretoria. Two civilians were killed. Then there was an attack on the Booysens Police Station. In retaliation, the SADF attacked the Chifufua ANC base in Angola, destroying it.

Bombs damaged railway lines at Dube, near Soweto, and grenades were thrown at the West Rand Administrative Offices, injuring two civilians, And, still, the pressure was mounting, as newspaper reporters told the grim stories of these terrorist attacks.

By now, it was time for Khazimela's cell to get out of the country, but not before they had exploded bombs at two critical power stations, their most dangerous being a rocket attack on the *Voortrekkerhoogte*[129] Military Base. It was now time for the next *uMkhonto we Siz*we cell group to come and wreak havoc in the country, to make it ungovernable, and to scare the population.

Khazimela, Sandile, and the other four made their way back to Zambia along the now well-known Freedom Pipe!

---

[129] Afrikaans word for 'Pioneer Heights'.

Chapter 19

For a moment or two, there was an eerie silence in the place of worship. The sun was now at its midday zenith, and the heat was becoming noticeable because there was no ceiling in the church. In fact, there was a 'click' here and a 'click' there as the zinc roof expanded due to the sun beating down on it. This added to the conspicuous silence.

Just then, there was a loud bang, and I ran to the window to see what had caused the noise. A big bird had landed on the roof, and it was now preening itself. I am sorry to say that I cursed the bird for giving me a fright!

I couldn't but think how easily the world could explode into action, and just how easily I had let down my guard, thinking all was safe!

It wasn't long before I heard the bird squawk loudly and take off again, obviously in search of its prey, and someone else to terrify!

Days at the SABC were great from a productive and creative point of view, but if you were the bearer of a name like Porter-Smith and did not vote for the National Party, the chance of any promotion, was highly doubtful. The broadcasting corporation was not known for its abundant salaries so after four years, David was obliged to seek other employment in the engineering field.

Equally, it was time for him to marry his very dear and

long-standing friend, Sarah-Jean, and the marriage soon resulted in the birth of two children, a girl, Paula, and a boy, Sean.

The year 1974 saw a general election, and this meant that opposition parties would have to do something extraordinary to shake the stronghold of the National Party. The United Party swung into action and elected a new leader, Harry Schwartz. The Porter-Smith family, along with thousands of other English-speaking people rallied their friends together and had various meetings, and endless cake sales, to raise party funds. They believed that this election would be different, apartheid would be stopped, and all reasonable people would simply mix easily with other races. But that was a pipe dream! The hard right-wing joined the fray, winning 4% of the vote, and the ultra left-wing, the New Progressive Party, under Colin Eglin won 5.3% of the vote.

David and the family were devastated to find that New Zealand had placed a sporting ban on South Africa. This would seriously affect watching Sunday afternoon games of rugby between the All Blacks and the Springboks, and of course, the many accompanying *braais* that would take place all over the country, mainly in the White suburbs.

At this time, David was involved in the citizen force of the SADF, and the international news of the Portuguese pulling out of their colonies of Angola and Mozambique was the topic of discussion and interest. After all, the incumbent rulers in both colonies were strongly backed by Russia, under the leadership of Brezhnev. It was no secret that during those so-called 'cold war' years, Russia was looking for interests in Africa, so Angola and Mozambique were good pickings!

The South African government kept a very close eye on the

situation, Angola in particular, when it was discovered that Cuba, a puppet state of Russia, had sent troops into that country. When the South African Army Intelligence was called in to assess the threat so close to the South West African border, it was no surprise that South Africa engaged the Cubans, full on, at a town called Ebo, not too far from the capital city of Luanda.

Later that same year, David was due to undergo his normal three-week citizen force training camp. He packed his kit bag, said goodbye to his family, and embarked on his training camp in Potchefstroom. But America's secretary of state, Henry Kissinger, had other ideas. He had secret talks with the South African government about Russia's expansion interests, and the deal was fairly simple. Through the auspices of the CIA, America would back South African troops, in a war against Angola and its Russian/Cuban backers.

The South African government agreed. After all, the SADF was undoubtedly the strongest army on the African continent, and to deal with a Cuban threat, particularly with American backing, would be a walk in the park. The news of the collusion soon filtered through to the troops in the training camp, and the three-week camp saw David, and thousands of others, having their time extended from weeks to months.

The push into Angola and the fight against Cuba/Russia had begun. South Africa was committed. As the SADF units went north and got closer to the capital, Luanda, winning battle after battle, the unthinkable happened. Kissinger and America withdrew their support, apparently because of America's failing success in Vietnam! South Africa was on her own and therefore decided to make a calculated withdrawal from Angola. This was to be a slow process, and many battles would still have to take place. Slowly, the SADF would pull out its main conventional forces, and replace them over the next years, with anti-terrorist forces.

Back at home, David was travelling to work one morning in Johannesburg. It was fairly early, and he turned his car onto the Ben Schoeman Highway, which split into a double-decker highway once it reached the outskirts of Johannesburg, with the south-bound traffic travelling on the upper level, while north-bound traffic drove on the lower level.

It had just gone seven-thirty when the news came on the radio, "Headline news," said the announcer. "Soweto is going up in flames! Children are rioting. Police are fighting running battles with school children in the township!"

David, who was now on the top section of the highway, looked across to the south west, and sure enough, smoke was billowing from the distinctive area of Soweto. Soon the highway turned to the left, and the view was gone. When he got to his office, he listened to the radio for any further news. There was none for the moment, but as the day progressed, so the news came of events taking place just a few kilometres away! Police, fire brigades, and ambulance vehicles could be heard, as their sirens echoed off the faces of nearby buildings.

Night came; many children had died, and many others were detained. The reason for the uprising was a bit blurred, but it appeared from local news reports that the Sowetan children were protesting because they refused to be taught through the medium of Afrikaans.

The United Party was at the time dissolving and could offer little, or no, assistance. However, in 1977, when the general election was held, the United Party, which had by then dissolved, formed the New Republic Party. David's mother,

Betye, was approached by this newly formed party, to stand for election against Helen Suzman of the Progressive Party, who held the parliamentary seat for Houghton. Betye declined.

And so, with the Soweto riots still fresh in the minds of the White electorate, the elections were held, and almost predictably, the National Party achieved a landslide victory. What was of definite interest though, was the sharp move to the left. The Progressive Party became the official opposition, the New Republic Party didn't do very well, and the HNP failed to win any seats. David explained to his family one evening, that it was interesting to note that the entire vote was controlled by just over one million White voters. The rest of the population had no say!

B J Vorster was the Prime Minister, but not for long, as P W Botha would soon take over that position, while Vorster would become the State President.

Later that year, in May, the SADF conducted a major operation in Angola, called Operation Cassinga. Although David wasn't part of the action, he followed it closely at headquarters. During the same year, the SADF attacked, and destroyed, a major South West African Peoples' Organisation (SWAPO) base.

In the foothills of the Magaliesberg mountain range, not far from Hartebeespoort Dam, there is a strange set of buildings called Pelindaba. Most people would drive past without taking any notice, but David's glance fell on a newspaper article, with a headline that read, 'First Nuclear Weapon'. He read on that South Africa was on the brink of manufacturing a nuclear bomb. *Fantastic news*, he thought. South Africa would be the first on the continent to have such a weapon! *Now we can show the world a thing or two*! he thought proudly. *Stuff the United*

Nations arms embargo and the Arabs with their oil embargo! By 1979, when South Africa, with the help of Israel, successfully tested a nuclear device in the southern part of the Atlantic Ocean, the world sat up and took notice!

Another report in the English papers was of the ANC base at Nova Catenque that had been attacked and destroyed, but it was overshadowed by the article on the Republic becoming a nuclear-equipped country.

As 1979 rolled into 1980, radio, television, and newspapers were filled with reports on terrorist attacks on government facilities and some even on civilian installations, like the bank at Silverton. The result of all this was that the ordinary English-speaking man in the street was becoming hardened to the plight of the Black man, and sympathy for the Black cause was running low. Polarization of the middle-class White population was evident. Folk were simply tired of reading and hearing about these bomb blasts.

The full-scale war effort of the SADF in Angola had evolved into attacks on specific bases. With the help of the UNITA[130] Forces in South East Angola, the attack on the Chifufua base was a prime example. Still, the hardening of attitudes, especially amongst White conscripts, was more and more evident. Troops were called up to three-week duties in the Black townships, which were boring and monotonous, simply fuelling the fires of resentment even more.

It wasn't surprising when Rhodesia broke diplomatic ties with the Republic. This news caused a stir, but was soon forgotten! What did, however, make sense in the English community was the abolishment of the Senate in Cape Town.

---

[130] The National Union for the Total Independence of Angola was founded in 1966 and is the second-largest political party in Angola.

South Africa's parliamentary system had always had a lower and an upper house in the Assembly, based on the original British system. Instead, the government announced the formation of what they called the President's Council, made up of 60 Whites, and a selection of appointed Indian and coloured representatives. Their task was to formulate a possible constitution.

At last, something positive was happening! In Afrikaans-speaking circles, it was felt that this was giving into the demands of the terrorists. In Black circles, it was just a white wash, as there were no Blacks included in the drawing up of the proposed constitution. Unrest in the townships increased, and patrolling by soldiers increased as well.

David explained to his family, once more, that it was never the intention of the government to give Blacks a say because they would soon have their homelands, where they could make their own policies, and write their own constitutions, providing they met with the rules of the White government.

On the eastern border of the Republic, terrorists were getting through, and the White soldiers were called upon to close the gap. At the United Nations, South Africa laid complaints about her borders being violated, but nobody listened because they were completely obsessed by the fact that South Africa could easily become a state with nuclear capabilities.

Pressure on the South African government grew, both internationally and from within, and the first calls of "Release Mandela!" started to make the news. Some people remembered the name from the Rivonia trial, but some even asked who this person was!

Early the following year, the homeland of KwaNdebele

became self-governing, and the Ciskei announced independence. Maybe this was the right answer! In the elections that year, the National Party won 131 of the possible 165 seats.

At Matola, in Mozambique, 12 ANC members were killed in a SADF raid. Forty ANC terrorist attacks were recorded, with 630 arrests being made. The world did not like what was happening, and this resulted in the United Nations calling for sanctions against South Africa to get the country out of South West Africa.

Hearts were hardened; Black people were frustrated, disappointed, and angry! The Afrikaners, but not all of them, were putting their hope in the government, which had recently released a statement that the twenty years between the start of the Republic and the present, could be considered the 'Golden Era'. David thought to himself, *They must be mad*!

By the end of that year, the SADF, together with UNITA, controlled a very large portion of south-eastern Angola. In South Africa, at least two million isiXhosa-speaking people received citizenship to the independent homeland known as Ciskei, under the first President of Ciskei, Chief Cebe.

David and his fellow conscripts continued to patrol the local townships, always on the lookout for terrorist activities and social unrest.

Chapter 20

I realised from my encounter with the noisy bird that had landed on the roof that I had immediately gone into fight or flight mode with the adrenalin still pumping in my body. I had unconsciously looked for a place to take refuge.

This immediately reminded me that there is a certain safety in numbers. Safety with like-minded people. If their philosophy is in sync with ours or not really doesn't matter much. The point is, there is safety in numbers.

This herd mentality is often sad; it doesn't permit any individual thought and always allows the lowest common denominator to take precedence over those with better and more progressive thoughts. But that's the way it has been for millennia and will be for many years to come. Why should our beloved country be any different?

The pressure was mounting for Sarel and his family, and many others who spoke Afrikaans, as they faced a predicament. The threat of the rise of the Black man lay heavily on their hearts. What would become of them? What would happen to their children? All these questions were raised in family chats each day.

The result was a hardening of attitudes and a typical laager mentality reaction. This laager stance came as a historical outcome of the Battle of Blood River, fought many, many years ago. It meant drawing together a circular barricade – in the original case, ox wagons – around those affected. Bring everyone of similar thought and mind into this protective circle, and fight together as a closed unit. This was the time for the Afrikaner to consolidate and put up a united front to the world.

Over the next fifteen years or so, this mentality would prevail, and it wasn't helped by the fact that small, enlightened groups were calling for the release of Nelson Mandela from prison. The laager effect kicked in immediately, and Black newspapers were immediately closed down and banned. A tit-for-tat response occurred in 1980 when *uMkhonto we Sizwe* struck at the huge Sasol petroleum plant in Secunda.

The next year saw another general election, and Sarel was delighted that the National Party won with a huge majority, under the control of P W Botha. Sarel, was in conversation with Sarel junior when the topic of an ultra-right-wing group called the Afrikaner Weerstand[131] Beweging[132] (AWB) led by Eugene Terblanche, was gaining momentum. According to Sarel, the Nationalist Party government were getting 'te sag'[133] on the Blacks.

The General Assembly of the United Nations was passing more and more sanction resolutions against South Africa, and overseas goods were becoming very costly and hard to come by in certain cases. F W de Klerk had replaced Treurnicht, as leader of the Transvaal constitution of the National Party parliament. "Pas op vir hierdie man!"[134] advised Sarel one evening, as he had his *dop*.

Later the same year, on 29 May 1983, White sentiment was

---

[131] Afrikaans word for 'Resistance'.
[132] Afrikaans word for 'Movement'.
[133] Afrikaans for 'too soft'.
[134] Afrikaans for 'Watch out for this man!'

again boosted, when 19 people were killed by a bomb, placed at the South African Air Force headquarters in Lyttelton. This attack, like all the others, drove the Whites into a frenzy of nationalism, and when the next general election came around, Sarel, his family, and many others would vote the mainly Afrikaans National Party back into office.

To secure the government position, the office of Prime Minister and the one of State President, were replaced by one office only, that of State President, under the incumbent, PW Botha. To put the icing on the cake, a state of emergency was declared in July 1985, giving the State President and his government extra-ordinary powers of control and detention. "Nou het ons hulle!"[135] declared Sarel over Sunday lunch.

But the English newspapers gave the call, once again, to release Nelson Mandela, and to stop the forced removal of Blacks from areas to make way for White settlement. One day, while Sarel was watching television, the announcer stated that the State President would soon be making a speech to the nation. Television crews from all over the world converged on Durban, as it had been leaked that the President would be making apartheid concessions, and some reconciliation remarks were expected.

The day of the speech to the nation arrived, and Sarel, along with many thousands of others, were glued to their seats, and their television sets. Was this the turning point of the conflict? Would this be the ceasing of unnecessary slaughter? The State President stepped up to the podium to address the world media, and the world held its breath!

He started speaking, and this anticipated speech just reinforced National Party thinking. The media, in general, were

---

[135] Afrikaans for 'Now we have them!'

lambasted; the world and its leaders were criticized. The non-release of Nelson Mandela was explained in detail. He ended his speech with these words, "I believe that we are today crossing the Rubicon. There can be no turning back." He went on to say that all would be well. The president had missed a golden opportunity. Instead, he had done the opposite, in world opinion. As a result, in that year, 1985, the interest rate rocketed to 25%; the inflation rate climbed to 16% and the bombings and killings escalated.

Sarel junior was part of the police group sent to raid the English newspaper offices. It was 1987 and time once again for another general election. Sarel and the White population voted, but this time Sarel voted for the right-wing Conservative Party, and he was amazed, when this new party received 26% of the seats in parliament, reducing the National Party seats to 52%, and the Progressive Party gained 14%. These results gave the National Party a scare. The swing to the right was notable, and the smaller, but important, swing to the left only ended up polarizing the White population, even more.

Meanwhile, on the streets of South Africa, bombs were killing more and more people. Limpet mines were being smuggled across the borders and into reaching the hands of *uMkhonto we Sizwe* cadres, who were using them to maximum effect. Land mines were now blowing up innocent individuals on indiscriminate roads in rural areas, and the latest device was that of car bombs. These devices knew no skin colour, and the result was the maiming and killing of many South Africans.

The Nordic countries joined in the sanctions against South Africa, and they became very vocal in their dislike of all things South African, pulling out of businesses, church missions, and anything else they were involved in.

Then, the unthinkable happened! A group of Afrikaner intellectuals broke ranks and had a secret meeting with the ANC leadership, in Dakar. Sarel felt that this was the ultimate betrayal to his Afrikaans-speaking brothers. How could his people go and talk to the enemy? The very people who were setting off bombs, and who were responsible for the killing of his people?

In response to the news, came an answer from the ultra-right-wing in the form of one individual, whose code name was 'Wit Wolf' (White Wolf). He simply went into the main square of the capital, Pretoria, and using a pistol he opened fire, killing nine Blacks, and wounding many more. The right-wing felt that this was more like it! Rather than talking, take action! The event, once again, polarised the population.

Just as Sarel junior was getting back to a fairly normal work schedule, an announcement came on the Television and in the newspapers that P W Botha, had suffered a minor heart attack, and would be handing over to Chris Heunis; he would still hold the reins as State President. The world asked if this was divine intervention. Perhaps, it was because in the election called just two years later, the National Party only won 48% of the seats in Parliament. The Democratic Party received a very useful 20%, but the surprise was the significant rise in the votes gained by the right-wing Conservative Party, which got 31% of the votes. To the enlightened thinker, this was very concerning!

Sarel and his cronies were delighted that their new ultra-right-wing party had at last gained momentum, and it would not allow the collapse of White and Black segregation. But, just as the Van Wyk family and their friends were feeling more relaxed about their position, under a new Conservative Party government, the formidable pair of Ministers FW de Klerk, and

Pik Botha, out-manoeuvred Chris Heunis, and the ailing P W Botha.

F W de Klerk took over the reins of government in the nick of time! Completely against the wishes of the party faithful, he announced the transition to end apartheid, the unbanning of the ANC, PAC, and the Communist Party, and the imminent release of Nelson Mandel.

At a braai, which Sarel organised for his family and like-minded friends, much discussion took place about the way De Klerk had sacrificed the Afrikaans-speaking people on the altar of Black expectations. Sarel senior, now 89 years old, encapsulated the whole situation with these words, "Ons is nou diep in die kak!"[136] Everyone at the braai agreed. They needed to rally around their leaders, and again form a laager!

By 1991, school segregation had been stopped. Black children were to be admitted to White government schools under the new 'Model C' plan. This system allowed for greater powers and authority for school governing bodies, who could run the school to suit their needs. Those who couldn't afford the fees were allowed to apply for a subsidy.

All people in South Africa were placed on a common population register. To the excitement of many, South Africa was once again invited to be part of the world-wide Olympic movement.

Sarel junior was about to turn 65, and that meant he could apply for retirement from the SAPS. He had had enough! He had seen far too many terrorist attacks on society and had witnessed too many innocent people, both Black and White, being killed. It was time for him to allow his children and his grandchildren to take over. He could see that it was only a

---

[136] Afrikaans for 'We are now deep in the shit!'

matter of time before he would become redundant as a White policeman. So, he decided to take his pension and sit back after so many years serving his country. This thought was further confirmed, when he learnt from his son, Paul, that Black children had already been enrolled at the school his grandchildren attended.

The White electorate was invited to vote in a referendum to decide whether all these pro-Black reforms were in order. The Van Wyk family, and many others, voted against it, but the vote carried and F W de Klerk's government moved quickly to bring about the changes.

The extreme right-wing did everything possible to stop the reforms. They had Chris Hani, the leader of the Communist Party, assassinated. At the time, during the delicate bi-lateral peace talks, this assassination was the worst thing that could have happened! South Africa was balancing on a knife edge! It was only the wise words of De Klerk, Mandela (who had been released from prison in 1990) and Tutu, that steadied the boat. As a collective thank-you, the world awarded De Klerk and Mandela, jointly, the Nobel Peace Prize. Arch Bishop Desmond Tutu had received his a few years earlier.

There was no turning back after that! The State of Emergency was lifted, and in the early part of 1994, the new and elaborate South African Constitution was debated and agreed upon by all signatories. A new flag was designed, and the National Anthem was adjusted, to include more of the ethnic languages, besides English and Afrikaans. The stage was set for the first, completely democratic, and free election, to take place in April 1994.

Sarel Van Wyk senior, had turned 94, but he didn't vote!

Chapter 21

Cruelty and hate for one's enemy know no bounds when it comes to planning another inhumane attack on innocent people. In military terms, it is normally referred to as co-lateral damage. After all, civilians do get in the way!

So often, the root cause of striking at the enemy in the first place is soon forgotten, and the revenge attacks become the order of the day! This escalation is like a runaway fire, it is almost impossible to stop, no matter how hard one tries to heal the original wound.

Days turn into weeks, months into years and still, the fight is fuelled. A target here, a bombing there, it's all part of the choreography of the battle dance. An explosion here, a few more people slaughtered there, the show goes on, each act more desperate than the one before!

At a break, the audience shuffles a little in their seats and tries hard to work out who is winning, or whose side should they be on, but sadly there are no winners, only losers!

Khazimela and his comrade Sandile made their way back successfully to the ANC training camp in Zambia, even though they had come pretty close, on two occasions, to police, and SADF units on the border.

The two were thoroughly debriefed and congratulated for all the targets they had attacked. Khazimela was now 52 years old, and the ANC hierarchy felt that he was now too old to continue the active guerrilla duties that he had done, and instead, his talents could be better used within the party, in exile. He thanked his superiors and vowed that he would serve *uMkhonto we Sizwe* well in their future plans.

Over the last few years, and with his age creeping up on him, he felt that it was time to marry. He had met Akhona, a lovely young woman, at the camp in Tanzania, some years before. They had kept up a somewhat disjointed relationship all the days that he had been on active service back in the Republic. She was known at the camp in Zambia, and Khazimela quickly took advantage of being with her.

The two exchanged their vows in front of the camp's senior officer, and the pair were technically married with a promise that as soon as South Africa was liberated, they would have a formal wedding with their families and friends at home. Little did they know that many years would pass before this could be realised. In the meantime, that did not stop their romance from blooming, and soon a baby boy, Bongani, was born. His name meant 'thankful' because his father was thankful for his birth in his senior years! Nine months later, a baby girl, Babalwa, meaning 'grace' was born.

Khazimela, now part of the operations cluster, ordered a bomb attack on the two nuclear electrical generating facilities at Koeberg. The rationale for this was that such a hit, particularly on a nuclear operation, would be a huge prize in the terrorist bombing attacks! Koeberg withstood the blast, and in retaliation, a bomb was successfully detonated at the ANC offices in the United Kingdom. This was a great cause for concern for Khazimela and his comrades back in Southern Zambia as there was ever-rising animosity between Xhosa followers of the ANC and the Zulu-supported Inkhata Freedom

Party (IFP).

This animosity was to become a massive challenge because the ANC automatically felt that all Black allegiance should be for the ANC, and the ANC only! It wasn't so, and in a lot of disputes, it was the IFP against ANC – 'Black on Black violence' as it was reported in the media. One such immediate case that came to Khazimela's attention was a bomb blast that killed four Council of South African Trade Unions (COSATU) members, outside Kagiso. At the time, COSATU was a labour council with deep sympathies for the ANC and its affiliates.

Khazimela and his group had a bigger project to deal with. The ANC in exile in Europe had requested, through diplomatic channels, that the president of Zambia, Kenneth Kaunda, should meet with the South African President P W Botha, aboard a train parked on the railway bridge over the Zambezi River, the border between Zambia and Southern Rhodesia.

The meeting took place but very little progress was made, and so the death and destruction continued. There were two more attacks on Koeberg, and bombs were detonated at the South African nuclear facility at Pelindaba. Various skirmishes took place on the Botswana border, the United Democratic Front (UDF) was launched in South Africa, and the ANC stirred up unrest in many of the mines.

South Africa was slipping into chaos! The answer was a state of emergency, which was declared, giving the police extraordinary powers to arrest and detain. Khazimela, took note of a slight softening of relations when the government announced the ceasing of forced removals, but this wasn't enough in the eyes of the ANC. However, there was the worrying aspect of Black-on-Black violence!

Added to this, were the ever-present ANC traitors, who

became informers for the police, and so the practice of 'necklacing' was set in motion. The practice was fairly straightforward. Once a traitor had been identified and apprehended, an old tyre was put around their necks, with a cup of petrol being placed in the tyre, and then it was set alight. This would be the fate of many who defied the 'movement'.

The police, with their powers under the state of emergency, tracked down small groups of terrorists and, without any formal authority, would eliminate these bands of Guerrillas. These acts brought about much speculation in the media, and the various terrorist groups replied by bombing places where civilian Whites would normally congregate. The Wimpy in Rissik Street was a prime example, and limpet mines were also detonated at the Devonshire Hotel in Braamfontein. These attacks on civilian targets, instead of government buildings, would be the new tactic of *uMkhonto we Sizwe*, overseen by Khazimela and his comrades in far-off Zambia.

Once again, Khazimela's expertise was put to the test when a group of Afrikaans-speaking intellectuals approached the ANC for a secret meeting with their leaders in exile. This came as a surprise to the leadership, but of course, they agreed that any approach would be helpful; the success of this meeting was never confirmed. News of the meeting resulted in an attack on the ANC offices in Gaborone, by the SADF, and the ANC insurgents introduced car bombs to their arsenal.

Black-on-Black violence was growing, as the IFP and the ANC, jostled for position. The IFP were at an advantage because their organization had not been banned. The ANC answered this with another attack on civilians, at a Wimpy restaurant.

1987 rolled over into 1988, with the papers full of ghastly

attacks on targets, and Black-on-Black violence was reported daily, particularly in the right-wing newspapers. Then the news broke that State President P W Botha had suffered a mild heart attack. Khazimela and his cadres celebrated through the night. 'Die Groot Krokodil'[137] was going to retire from active duty, but would remain the State President.

The state of affairs was short-lived because on 20 September, F W de Klerk was sworn in as the new State President, and this took the ANC by surprise. This man had been a minister in parliament and was a much younger man, but the ANC knew little about him, or his attitude towards the Black majority.

They didn't have to wait long! The political prisoners on Robben Island were released, and early in the new year, it was time for Khazimela and his wife Akhona, to leave the base in Zambia, and return home to the Republic. Their two children, Bongani and Babalwa, would come home at the end of the next year when they completed their studies in the UK along with other exiled children.

The first week or so back home was very difficult for Khazimela and his wife. He looked over his shoulder everywhere he went, petrified that an informer or the police would recognise him. Finding appropriate accommodation was also a major problem. However, when the children returned home the following year, the family moved into their new home in Dobsonville, in Soweto.

The honeymoon with Dobsonville was soon over when gunmen opened fire on ANC mourners at a funeral service, in a church not far from where the family lived. The family

---

[137] Afrikaans for 'The Big Crocodile'.

152

discussed their future in South Africa and the safety of their children, who had been born in exile and had little knowledge of family traditions in South Africa. They had both been enrolled in 'Model C' schools and were in the minority, as most of the children were White. The family decided to give things a fair try!

Khazimela, now sixty-two years of age, had no commercial experience, and could not find employment. Ahkona was luckier, as she found a position as an aid, at a retirement village in the Roodepoort area. As a result of his inability to get work, he decided to join the uMkhonto we Sizwe Veteran's Association, based in Soweto. The organisation tasked itself with dealing with the needs of returning guerrillas. It was not funded by the government, and so they had to fend for themselves. The first matter on the agenda was Black-on-Black violence. Their conclusion was always the same. How could Black brothers, Black comrades, turn against their own kind? In the ranks of the Veterans, it was felt that Whites were stirring up hatred between the ANC and IFP and that this was a third-party plot, to destabilise the delicate political situation.

Black-on-Black violence continued. An IFP counsellor was shot dead, and the jockeying for Black power continued. To the cheers of millions, the end of apartheid was announced, and Nelson Mandela was released. He flew to Sweden, to meet with Oliver Tambo and the ANC governors in exile. As a gesture of goodwill, and in the spirit of reconciliation, *uMkhonto we Sizwe* announced the end to hostilities.

But, still, the fighting between the Xhosa and the Zulu continued, resulting in the death of some five hundred people. Parliament passed the scrapping of racial segregation, and for the first time since the early fifties, Khazimela and his comrades sat down at an ANC conference in Johannesburg.

Then came the staggering news that 55 ANC members had been killed at a funeral in Senekal. A curfew was placed on Black townships after another group of political rivals had been killed. In June of the same year, 46 IFP and ANC members, were killed at the hostel in Boipetong. A new word was now spreading by the media, that a 'Third Force' was to blame.

This unknown 'Third Force' was blamed for all the ensuing Black-on-Black violence. Nobody came forward, and no group claimed responsibility, but still, the killings went on unabated. Then, just as the Third Force was being blamed for many unknown killings, the Ciskei Defence Force, opened fire on a crowd at Bisho, killing twenty-nine people.

Azanian Peoples' Liberation Army (APLA) claimed five attacks, killing scores of people in King Williamstown, at the local golf club; at the Hillcrest Hotel in East London; a police station in Dobsonville; and at a tavern in Heidelberg. Eleven White worshippers were killed as they knelt in prayer in St James Church in Kenilworth, a suburb in Cape Town. To Khazimela and the returning exiles, this was a huge blow to their efforts towards creating a political solution. It was one they had not anticipated and had no idea how to stop it.

Many ANC delegations met with rival groups, but it all culminated in yet another massacre between ANC and IFP supporters at Escort. The South African government declared a state of emergency, this time in KwaZulu-Natal[138], once again giving extraordinary powers to the authorities. The only solution lay in the ANC and the IFP hammering out their differences at a conference table. Khazimela was part of this delegation, but the conference could not come to an agreement,

---

[138] Present-day name for 'Natal'.

and the situation was at a deadlock! However, a secret meeting between ANC representatives and King Goodwill Zwelithini of the Zulus was arranged by Mangosuthu Buthelezi of the IFP, which halted the killings, and the talks with the White government went ahead.

The South African government representatives and Khazimela, with his ANC cadres, were still determined to meet, and after much debate, the period of 27–29 April 1994 was set aside for the first democratic elections in the country.

Fundile, Khazimela's father, voted for the first time in the first Democratic elections! He had celebrated his 94th birthday just a few days earlier.

Chapter 22

The Holy Scriptures talk about the tongue being mightier than the sword, and I am sure that had there been any press in that time period, the Scriptures would have added something about the press being more powerful than a firearm!

But as the battle raged for the mind of the ordinary man, the warring parties realised that guns and bombs, alone, were not sufficient to level the war! And so, new words became commonplace – words like economic sanctions and arms embargos came to the printing presses. These were applied, and a whole new industry was immediately born. Things like sanction busters, and illegal and foreign arms dealers suddenly appeared.

Of course, sanctions hurt, but they hurt the poor man in the street the most and cleverly avoided those for whom it was meant.

International companies packed their bags and moved out, leaving thousands of people without an income. Brother turned on brother because of their sheer desperation. Nothing was going as per the script, and the lowly man had to bear the brunt!

The sun outside my place of worship had now passed its zenith and arched its way to the west. A tiny patch of mid-afternoon sun peeped through the window on the opposite side of the room. Was this a sign that the heat, or the conflict, was now over, and the pinnacle had at last been reached? Was this flash of sunlight on the western pane that ray of hope for better things to come?

South Africa had become the laughing stock, and whipping boy, of the world. Sanctions were crippling the economy, and petrol and other commodities were being rationed in some instances. A South African Navy frigate had sunk after colliding with the SAS *Tafelberg*, killing sixteen sailors.

The company that David worked for gave up on ideas of expanding their business into neighbouring countries. The talk everywhere was of complete doom and gloom. White male conscription was at its highest, and White youngsters in mine-proofed vehicles were seen patrolling the Black townships daily.

Opposition parties tried to table a no-confidence vote against P W Botha but to no avail! The whole situation was a ticking time-bomb, and no one in the northern suburbs of Johannesburg could work out why the government could not at least open up talks with the ANC. The popular thought was that this would at least buy the country some time.

Little notice was accorded to a newspaper article that a certain F W de Klerk was replacing the right-wing Andries Treurnicht as the leader of the National Party in the Transvaal Province. However, there was some hope in a report that P W Botha was to meet the president of Zambia in a railway coach on the border between Zambia and Southern Rhodesia.

South African cartoonists had a field day, depicting the South African President, wagging his finger at President Kaunda, and that president, swatting the flies with his fly swatch. All of this was in an attempt to solve the occupation of South West Africa by the Republic. Most people thought that the two would include some discussion on the internal affairs of the Republic, but they didn't! It was completely taboo to discuss the internal affairs of the country with a foreign president. The result of this coach meeting was nothing but fair game for the press! "Who is kidding who?" David stated at dinner one evening while eating his roast chicken.

What it did bring, was the reaction to criticism, of an attack by the SADF on ANC offices in Maseru. Surprisingly, the Lesotho government did not object too loudly, and inter-governmental talks began on the building of what was to become the Lesotho Highlands Water Scheme. This was to be a multi-million water project, that would supply water to the Vaal River System, which in turn, would supply water to the industrial heartland of the Transvaal, particularly to Johannesburg and the immediate surrounds. In return, Lesotho, the completely landlocked mountain kingdom, would receive substantial monthly payments from the Republic. So, when the raid on the ANC offices in Maseru happened, no wonder little was said! South Africa needed the vast water supply and Lesotho would receive foreign currency – and a lot of it!

Later that year, the papers were once again filled with pictures of dead and bloodied people after a bomb attack on the South African Air Force Head Quarters in Pretoria. This attack had a special impact on David, as a good friend, lost his eyesight in the attack. It was no surprise then that the SADF launched 'Operation Askari' consisting of hundreds of troops.

Try as hard as they might the English-speaking vote was denied at the 1984 election polls. But more worrying for them, was the apparent rise in votes for the right-wing Conservative Party. This could only spell disaster. However, a few months later, the government announced that they were withdrawing all troops from southern Angola. The conscripts drew a sigh of relief, even though they still had to patrol the townships.

There was little respite in the press from political goings on when it was reported that Lee McCall, of the Stander Gang, had been shot in the suburb of Houghton. For many months, this gang had been pursued after their many daring bank-heists. Andre Stander, the mastermind and leader of the gang, had met two other criminals, Allan Heyl and Lee McCall, in the Zonderwater Maximum Security Prison, where he was serving a sentence for bank robbery. The three men managed to escape and went on a spree of daring bank robberies. McCall was killed, Heyl captured and returned to prison, and Stander was pursued high and low, but was never caught in the country. He skipped to America, where he settled in Fort Lauderdale. He changed his identity, hoping to move to Australia, but was recognised and eventually taken down by the police. "And that is that!" David said to Sarah-Jean after he had read the report in the evening paper.

The relentless bombing of targets by *uMkhonto we Sizwe*, hardened the attitude of the general White population, and sympathy for the cause, was running out. The motivation for the senseless killings was being questioned by so many people.

Then suddenly, out of the blue, came the signing of the nKomati Accord, a non-aggression treaty between Mozambique, Portugal and South Africa. It was soon revealed that South Africa would sponsor, and build, a massive dam wall on the Zambezi River, at Cahora Bassa, which would house electric turbines. This hydro-electric plant would supply electricity, right into the heart of the industrial area called Olifantsfontein, halfway between Johannesburg and Pretoria. The rationale was the same – Mozambique needed the revenue, and South Africa needed the energy. The success of this agreement prompted P W Botha and Pik Botha to visit Europe, to plead South Africa's case.

Back in Angola, came the news that mutineers in the ANC Pango Camp had taken and killed all their own administrative staff. This did little towards helping the image of the ANC, as seen by the White public, back in South Africa. Letters coming to the training camps had to be scrutinised and carefully handled, as many were now filled with just enough explosives to blow off the hands of those opening them. The ANC's answer to this was the placing of more bombs in the Republic.

And still, the Black-on-Black threat grew, and in September 1984, at about the time that P W Botha was inaugurated as state president, ANC councillors were doused with petrol and set alight! News got out that South African diplomats were holding talks with the terrorist organization, called RENAMO,[139] and the ANC felt that their training camps in Mozambique could be in jeopardy.

The bombs and killings went on, to the point that the South African government declared a new state of emergency. A certain amount of reserved optimism was felt in the ranks of the ANC when, in 1985, P W Botha offered to release Nelson Mandela. Khazimela and his comrades noted that if this happened, Mandela would have to distance himself from the armed revolution, and all their work and planning would be for nothing. *Surely, Mandela would not agree to such terms*, was the thought of those in the camps in Zambia!

As a tantaliser, the South African government stopped the forced removal of Blacks, and Denis Goldberg, one of the

---

[139] From the Portuguese '*Resistênca Nacional Moçambicana*', Portuguese for 'Mozambican National Resistance'.

Rivonia Trialists, was released from prison after twenty-two years of incarceration. But Mandela declined the release and stayed on in prison.

The police were given extraordinary policing powers as a result of the state of emergency, and Khazimela and his planning teams had to direct their cadre operatives on the ground very carefully. He was informed that operatives in Gugulethu and Cradock had been summarily arrested, and had gone missing. Local newspapers referred to these people by the number in their group and thus spoke of the Gugulethu seven, the Cradock four, the Pebco three, and so on. This sent ripples of condemnation, and hate, through the rank and file of *uMkhonto we Sizwe*. Their base in Gaborone was attacked by the SADF, killing twelve of their members.

It was now full-on war! Thirty-six magisterial districts throughout South Africa were deemed special emergency areas. The bombing of an area known as Umlazi was authorised by *uMkhonto we Size*, and saw thirty Zulu children badly injured. This was just another instance of Black-on-Black violence. But this was not what the ANC hierarchy had in mind. Yes! Target the White man and his installations, but not cadres!

Somehow, ANC intelligence was getting into the hands of sympathisers. Some Blacks were thought to be traitors, so *uMkhonto we Sizwe* was given the go-ahead to carry out the so-called necklacing of these people. This diabolical method of burning someone to death, by putting a tyre around their neck, filling it with petrol and setting it alight, was indeed inhumane! This form of terrorism was useful in that it frightened the would-be traitors before they turned on their Black brothers.

Orders from the highest echelons to the camps in Zambia and Botswana were clear. Rockets, delivered from Russia, and anti-tank mines were to be used in the conflict. Limpet mines were easy to place, and trigger, so they were used wherever possible. Wimpy Restaurants were declared fair targets, and many patrons, mainly Whites, were killed. The terrorists were now on a roll, and the fact that the pass laws had been withdrawn, made for easier movement of those laying the mines.

1987 was to be yet another year of mayhem, all planned and executed by *uMkhonto we Sizwe*, from the countries to the north and north-west of South Africa. Then the strangest thing happened, as far as Khazimela was concerned. Completely out of the blue, an Afrikaans-speaking delegation of intellectuals met with Thabo Mbeki. Was this a softening of the enemy? Only time would tell.

Khazimela could not allow this respite to stop his teams from carrying out attacks, and the new tactic became one of car bombs that could carry more explosives and do far more damage to the target. Violence continued between IFP and ANC unabated. This was truly a scar on the ANC, and Nordic countries instituted sanctions against South Africa. Well-known brands were withdrawn from the market, and regular household brands suddenly left the country, leaving scores of people without work.

Back in the training camps in Zambia and Botswana, the news was received that was very worrying to the cadres. In July, the battle of Caleque in Southern Angola raged between the SADF and the Cubans. The SADF stationed there, showed its conventional war capabilities, which worried *uMkhonto we Sizwe* cadres, and so another hit was ordered on a Wimpy; this time killing one and injuring fifty-seven.

So impressive was the SADF attack on Caleque, that the

ANC started dismantling its bases in Angola. Soon after, Angola and Cuba signed an accord, which saw the withdrawal of Cuban forces from Angola and the final Independence of South West Africa.

Back at home, the Progressive Party, which had done so badly in the last election, merged with the Democratic Party, forming a stronger left-wing alliance. The newspapers reported the moving of Nelson Mandela from Robben Island to the Victor Verster prison in Cape Town.

Early in January the following year, Khazimela heard the news from South Africa, on his short-wave radio, and he called his fellow cadres. It was announced, that the hated leader of the White South African government, P W Botha, would be stepping down as the leader of the National Party, but would remain on as the State President. The partying and the cheering went on long into the night at the camps, but it would be months before anything solid would happen.

The orders from the ANC in exile still came through, and the orders were still the same – keep up the pressure! This was exactly what they did, and then, in July 1989, came the news that P W Botha would be meeting with Nelson Mandela. Already rumours were abounding, about P W's failing health, and that a new minister, Pik Botha, was about to make some changes. No one had any idea of what these would be.

In what seemed to be a roller-coaster ride of political events, that would be the topic of conversation in every home and every news item on television, Khazimela and others were surprised when on the twentieth of September, F W de Klerk was pronounced as the new South African State President. Who was this man? What would be his new tactic? The answer soon came, when in February 1990, many ANC prisoners were

163

released from Robben Island, and Nelson Mandela was separately released from Victor Vester prison in Cape Town. A new election date was announced, to test the position and policies of the government, under the leadership of De Klerk.

The election took place, De Klerk secured his position, and negotiations to end apartheid started. The ANC, PAC, and the Communist Party were unbanned, and the state of emergency was lifted. Oliver Tambo and Nelson Mandela met in Sweden after twenty-eight years.

It was now time for Khazimela and his wife to leave the Zambian base and return to South Africa. Their two children would come home at the end of the following year, after they had completed their studies in the UK, along with many other exiled children. The first week or so back at home was very difficult for Khazimela and Akhona, as he kept looking over his shoulder, petrified that an informer, or the police, would recognise him. Finding appropriate accommodation also proved to be a problem. The fighting was technically over, but the animosity was still there, even though racial segregation was a thing of the past.

It didn't help Khazimela's cause when in August, five hundred Xhosa and Zulus were killed in various bouts of infighting.

In the new year, Khazimela, his wife, and his children were reunited, and they moved into a newly acquired two-bedroom house in the suburb of Dobsonville, in Soweto, with a view to getting better accommodation later. After all, the cadres were promised great wealth and fortune while still in the camps outside the borders of South Africa.

But the honeymoon with Dobsonville was soon over when, one day, gunmen killed thirty-nine ANC mourners on their way to a funeral at a church in the suburb, not far from where the family lived. At dinner that night, the family discussed the future of their family in South Africa, and the safety of their children. One had to bear in mind that their two children, Bongani and Babalwa, had been born in exile, and had very little knowledge of family traditions invested in South Africa.

They were both at a new Model-C school and at the time they were in the minority from a Black point of view. But the family jointly agreed to give the new circumstances a fair try, if nothing else.

In the winter of the following year, just as the political landscape was developing, news came that members of the ANC and the IFP had attacked each other, resulting in the death of fifty-six people at Boipatong that day.

Khazimela was 62 years of age at this time, and although he held a degree in Political Science, gained during apartheid, it was now actually worthless. He had no commercial working experience and didn't know how he was going to earn a living. But he held on to the promise of wealth and fortune! His wife, Akhona, was a little more fortunate. She found work at a retirement village in the Roodepoort area.

As a result of his inability to get work, Khazimela joined the *uMkhonto we Sizwe* Veterans Association, based in Soweto. This organization tasked itself with dealing with the needs of the returning guerrillas. The organization was not funded by the government and had to find funds for itself.

September saw the massacre of another twenty-nine Black people when the Ciskei Defence Force opened fire on a crowd in what came to be known as the 'Bisho Massacre'. APLA joined in the killing and slaughtered four children at the golf course in King Williamstown.

The Black-on-Black violence and the killing of comrades were often discussed at Khazimela's veterans' society meetings. The conclusion was always the same. How could Black brothers, Black comrades who had been suppressed by the White majority for so many years, turn their weapons upon fellow comrades.

Soon, there was talk in the ranks of the veterans that White men were stirring up hatred between the ANC and the IFP and that this violence was a third-party plot to de-stabilise the talks that were slowly taking place. But this logic did not make sense when the veterans agreed that APLA was an independent Black organization. APLA killed five more Whites in East London but killed four Blacks at a police station in Dobsonville. This action confused the so-called Third-Force theory completely when, in June, 11 ANC and IFP members were killed at Estcourt in Natal, and one month later APLA killed eleven White worshippers as they knelt to pray at the St James Church in Kenilworth, in the city of Cape Town.

The year ended with APLA killing another four people at a tavern in Heidelberg. These killings were a huge embarrassment to the ANC hierarchy while they and the South African government tried to piece together a new dispensation for the Republic of South Africa. So bad were the killings that a state of emergency was again declared in the province of KwaZulu-Natal.

ANC and IFP talks deadlocked, and there were concerns that all the political progress that had been made to that point, would be scuppered. Luckily, a second meeting between the ANC and King Goodwill Zwelithini, of the Zulus, with the help of Mangosuthu Buthelezi, of the IFP, halted the killings, and the talks with the White government continued.

On 27 April 1994, Khazimela and Akhona, together with Kazimela's father, Fundile, now 94, went to the polls and cast their votes in the first democratic election.

Chapter 23

I hadn't realised how hard a pew could be on one's buttocks! Apart from getting up for a drink of water, nearly two hours ago, I thought I needed to give my butt a rest! I got up from what had now become 'my seat' on the pew and became aware of the relief as blood returned to my posterior. My hands also assisted with a good massage!

After walking up and down the aisle twice, I found a hand-crafted cushion laying on another pew, so I took it to sit on. Oh yes! That was much better!

It dawned on me that my thoughts had strayed most of the morning, from the prayers I had come to pray. I immediately apologised to the Almighty for straying from the task I had set myself. So, I put my hands together and continued to pray. "Please Lord," I prayed, "we have been through so much, surely the end of the turmoil must be in sight? Surely Khazimela and his family must realise that a new dispensation is a few weeks away! Dear Lord, the senseless killings need to stop!"

The constant patrolling of the Black townships by the White SADF conscripts was taking its toll on the physique of the youth and the economy. The economic success of the National Party government was in tatters. International sanctions were making an impact on the economy and the morale of businessmen, and so when an SA Navy frigate sank after colliding with the SAS *Tafelberg*, drowning sixteen sailors, the majority of the White English-speaking population had had enough!

A vote of no confidence was called by the opposition party, but this was heavily defeated by the ever-strong National Party. A little-known minister, F W de Klerk, was sworn in to replace Andries Treurnicht as leader of the National Party in the Transvaal province. Nobody took much notice of the political development.

Another non-event, in the eyes of the weary South African public, was the signing of a non-aggression pact with Swaziland. Who cared? After all, Swaziland was just a small independent country that relied heavily on South Africa for its income! What did appeal to those who had fought in South West Africa and Angola, was the news that P W Botha and Kenneth Kaunda of Zambia had met on the bridge over the mighty Zambezi River, to discuss the future of South West Africa. This was believed to be a step in the right direction; did South Africa need the burden of South West Africa, as well, while there was so much racial discord, and ongoing poverty in South Africa herself?

"Who is kidding who?" commented David at a dinner party, while eating his roast lamb!

But, still, the bombs went off, each time damaging government buildings and structures, and in December of that year, the SADF raided an ANC base in Maseru, just to tip the balance back in White South Africans' favour.

In the following April, the government announced their involvement in the Lesotho Highlands Water Project, which would see to the supply of water to the Vaal industrial area and Johannesburg for the next fifty or so years. It was a win-win situation for both countries, as Lesotho needed the money, and

South Africa needed the water because it is basically a dry region.

In that same April, the attack on SADF Headquarters in Pretoria left a very real taste of bitterness for David, as a friend of his had a quarter of his face blown away in the explosion that killed nineteen other people. The retaliatory strike didn't take long to happen. The SADF attacked and destroyed an ANC settlement in Maputo.

In November, the SADF launched Operation Askari, which hit terrorist bases very hard. But, then, just as quickly as the SADF arrived in Angola, as rapidly did they pull out. Mozambique, because of the raid on Maputo a few months earlier, approached the South African government, and the nKomati Accord was signed, agreeing to non-aggression from both sides. The treaty was a win for both countries, as it heralded the signing, and the starting, of the massive Cahora Bassa hydro-electric scheme, which would see a dam being built on the Zambezi River where it entered Mozambique. South Africa desperately needed the extra electricity supply, as did Mozambique, which also needed the revenue it would bring.

Was this the start of a new world relationship that PW Botha and Pik Botha had travelled to Europe to create? Was South Africa on a rising trajectory for a change?

Then came the talks with RENAMO in Mozambique, and it looked as if peace might still be an option. But the reality was different! The armed wing of the ANC, *uMkhonto we Sizwe*, set off bombs to explode; city councillors were doused with petrol and set alight. It was just too much, and to control it all, a general state of emergency was declared. Desmond Tutu, the Arch-Bishop of the Anglican Church in Cape Town, was awarded the Nobel Peace Prize, for his efforts to bring about peace, to a country that was tearing itself apart!

The year 1985 brought more than its fair share of misery and disillusionment. The government stopped the forced removal of Blacks from their properties, which the Nationalist Government thought would appease at least some of the tensions. It didn't! In June, the Headquarters of the Irish Regiment in Marshall Street was again bombed, but *uMkhonto we Sizwe* operatives were misguided, as citizen force members were not present at the time of the explosion.

Once again, the government offered to release Nelson Mandela, but he refused the offer because of conditions stipulating he would have to renounce violence. In reply and retaliation, the SADF attacked and killed 12 ANC cadres, at a camp in Gaborone.

In August of that year, the press announced that P W Botha was going to address the country, with what was thought to be a conciliatory speech, filled with new hope for an end to the terrorist war which had ravaged the country, and taken its toll on both Black and White people. But the speech that would become known as the 'Rubicon' speech, was exactly the opposite. He wagged his finger at the TV audience, and licked his lips, as he announced that his government would not give in to the demands of the terrorists; Nelson Mandela had refused his release, and there would now be no concessions at all!

The country went into freefall! The JSE closed its doors. The interest rate rose above 25%, and the value of the rand plummeted. With the rand value being at an all-time low, the pessimistic mood for the economy was hard to comprehend. Unemployment rose and work was hard to find. People were defaulting on their mortgage bonds, and the repayment of loans was virtually impossible, as people hardly had enough on which to survive. Banks were not giving loans without 100% collateral. Everything was doom and gloom.

In November 1986, David with a group of citizen force members and veterans was invited to the opening of the new monument in Delville Wood. The monument commemorated the Battle of Delville Wood during World War I, where hundreds of South African soldiers had fought against the Germans, to hold the forest area at Delville Wood. Many soldiers lost their lives in the battle. The original monument had been added to with funds from the South African government, and so on 11 November, Armistice Day, a contingent of serving men, veterans, and politicians flew to France to officiate at the opening of the memorial.

The affair was grand, but the reception of the South Africans, from other European countries, was hostile to say the least. Demonstrations were held wherever the men went, and at one of the hotels where they were staying, a bomb was detonated against the wall of the hotel doing very little damage to the building, but a three-storey glass façade, at an adjoining building, crashed to the ground. The South African contingent left France quickly and quietly.

Although the relationship between South Africa and Mozambique was cordial, and a working relationship had been established, it came as a huge surprise in 1989 when an aeroplane, carrying Samora Machel, the President of Mozambique, crashed into a mountain, just within South African territory. Questions abounded – was this an ordinary accident, or was there something more suspicious? Rumours were rife, and accusations very real. The Margo Commission was established to investigate the accident, and the outcome was that it had been a pilot and navigational error; the real truth was perhaps more evasive!

Back at Citizen Force HQ, news reached them of three soldiers killed in a township while travelling in a Hippo armoured vehicle. This patrolling was taking its toll on White conscripts.

In April of that year, White South Africans went to the polls once more. The feeling was that the right-wing National government would not do too well, as they had done so much harm to the country, and that the left-wing Progressive Party would do much better this time around. The more enlightened capitalists didn't see it coming, but the results were devastating. The National Party won the election by a very small margin, however, the shock came when it was announced that the ultra-right Conservative Party had ousted the Progressive Party, to become the new official opposition.

What went wrong? Why were some Whites, supporting the continuation of terrorist warfare? And so, it came as no surprise when twenty-three White conscripts refused to do military training, preferring jail instead, and were labelled 'conscientious objectors'. Other young White males were finding many excuses to leave the country, "in order to study" was what their parents told their friends!

The second largest Black political party was the IFP, and they had never been banned but had tried to work with the Nationalist government. So, when the Black-on-Black killings started, President F W de Klerk knocked on the door of Chief Mangosuthu Buthelezi, the leader of the party, intending to create peace talks, between Blacks who were disrupting the lives of so many.

Apartheid was dismantled, and a new multi-racial

constitution would be written. So, in 1991 the Convention for a Democratic South Africa (CODESA) talks would be held in Kempton Park. This pleased European countries, who promptly lifted sanctions, and the Olympic Management Committee invited the country to participate in the upcoming Olympic Games which would take place the following year. The USA also agreed to lift sanctions. "Things are starting to happen!" David said to his father one evening. Financial agencies were talking about a new financial future and the rand/dollar exchange rate looked much better on financial charts.

As part of the South West Africa settlement, Walvis Bay, a strategic port on the west coast was formerly handed over to the new Namibian government. F W de Klerk was starting to show his political muscle, and at the end of 1992, he dismissed twenty-three high-ranking military officers, including some generals, for disrupting negotiations with the ANC. Slowly but surely, he was gaining support from the moderate English-speaking public.

White Model-C schools were opened to admit Black learners. These previously all-White schools were managed by a School Governing Body (SGB) and they set the parameters for the admission of children of other races. Black parents clamoured to get their children into these schools. However, many of these schools did not have space for too many extra pupils, and schools that had to turn some children away, were often labelled 'racist'.

In 1993, the president admitted that the country did have nuclear capability, and this worried many international communities. But things fell apart once more, when an extreme right-wing operative, assassinated Chris Hani, leader of the Communist Party. Once again, the country was balancing on a knife edge. No one knew, no one could guess, which way or when the tide would turn. Fortunately, Nelson Mandela called for calm, and peace talks continued. But even his call didn't stop APLA's indiscriminate killings.

In October 1993, there was much celebrating when Nelson Mandela and De Klerk were jointly awarded the Nobel Peace Prize, for their efforts in trying to bring about peace in the country. The newspapers and television were filled with talks and more talks, negotiation after negotiation, and so when 1994 dawned, it was a new era for South Africa.

The Porter-Smith family celebrated on 27 April with thousands of other people of all races as they queued to cast their ballots in the first all-inclusive democratic election. Michael John would soon be 94!

The result was as expected. Nelson Mandela, of the ANC, was elected president of the Republic, and De Klerk and Thabo Mbeki, were joint deputies. The final arms embargo was lifted by the United Nations, and peace appeared to be on the horizon. So much so, that Queen Elizabeth and her entourage felt it was safe enough to visit the country after so many years.

To the delight of rugby fanatics and many others in the population, the match between New Zealand and the Springboks was played in the Rugby World Cup final, in the middle of the following year. The South African team beat their opponents, and this was the tonic that was needed at the time. The entire country celebrated, and Nelson Mandela, who was present at the match wearing his Springbok jersey, accepted the trophy, together with the captain of the team, Francois Pienaar. This momentous occasion was displayed all over the local and overseas press, and on television. The healing process had begun after nearly fifty-two years.

The scorecard was difficult to comprehend. 21,000 people died because of apartheid, between the years 1949 and 1994. Of this number, 14,000 were killed in the years 1990 to 1994, of which 92% was through Black-on-Black violence. It was time for the country to put the past behind it.

South Africa needed to know who had been responsible, and how people were going to be held accountable. So, it was agreed that the truth needed to be brought to the fore, and a Truth and Reconciliation Commission was set up, chaired by Desmond Tutu. The conditions were simple! Provided people were truthful, and held back no facts, the perpetrators would, generally, be pardoned, so that reconciliation could begin its healing process. It mostly worked well, and there were very few exceptions where the truth was not told.

A new era had dawned, in South Africa. Everyone was free. White dominance was over. Apartheid was at last dead! But was it?

Chapter 24

I stopped my prayer for just a second to realign my thoughts, and as I did, I noticed a butterfly flapping its wings, and settling on the flower of the pot plant on the window ledge. As I stared at it, I was amazed at the size of its wings, and just how delicately they were suspended on its back. It suddenly dawned on me that it must have flown in through the door that I had left open when I entered the church hours before.

I got up. Suddenly, this magnificent creature, created by God, was my responsibility. If I locked the building while it was still inside, it would surely die! I could not have that on my conscience. I wasn't sure how I was going to get it out, or how I was going to catch it without damaging its wings! Could I even get close enough to hold it in my hands?

I stopped two metres short of the butterfly and considered my options. Now, only a short distance away, I marvelled at its beauty – shades of red and orange, so carefully and identically matched on either wing. It appeared as if a tiny photocopier had copied one wing and placed the pattern on the other to match!

I thought that this Heaven that everyone talks about, and longs to stay in, must have dozens of butterflies just like this one.

All I could do was open wide the nearest window, trust that it would feel the breeze, and fly out. And that is exactly what happened! With a flap of its wings, it took off as if answering my prayer.

I sighed and said a thank you to God and returned to my seat on the pew. At least one of God's creatures would live to see another day!

Over the last 24 chapters, we have journeyed with Sarel Van Wyk, Fundile Khumalo, Michael John Porter-Smith, and their families. Hopefully, you have some idea of the three different perspectives, and circumstances, that have led the families to this point.

One could argue that the Khumalo family suffered the most during the years of White oppression and dominance, but it would also be reasonably true to state that everyone lived extraordinary lives, and that all three families lost almost a century to a government policy that brought tears and heartache to all concerned.

Based on the horrors of what was known as apartheid, it would seem that perpetrators as well as those on the receiving end would equally want to turn a completely new page of history and start afresh. But at the beginning of this book, we spoke about the 'half-life' of a substance. We spoke about the effectiveness of a pill reaching its peak so many hours after it was taken.

What you have read is only the 'half-life' of this story. The other 'half' is to follow…

The euphoria of the 1994 elections and the winning of the Rugby World Cup captured the attention of the rest of the world. A new multi-coloured flag was unfurled, an extension to the anthem was written, a fresh constitution was drawn up, and the country was known as 'The Rainbow Nation!' Everyone loved it!

The tide had turned, and nothing was holding the country back! The entire country was running like a well-oiled machine, after years and years of trade embargos, sanctions, hostilities and demonstrations. The economy picked up and was ticking over. Hospitals, both private and government, were working well and the rail, air, and transport systems were slick operations. Municipalities were serving their constituencies with all the necessary services, such as lighting, water and sanitation.

In short, South Africa was able to look after, feed, and employ its population. At the time of taking over, the new government was handed a fully operational and corruption-free, working unit! It goes without saying that because of the apartheid system, and its legacy, many had been excluded from the lifestyles that the minority enjoyed.

But here was an opportunity to rebuild, and make sure that everybody, without exception, could share in the bounty of the New South Africa! However, the pill had only reached half of its lifecycle!

Chapter 25

I had returned to my seat with relief, after letting the magnificent butterfly out of the window, to continue with its life.

It seemed obvious to me that this was my cue to say thank you to God for a wonderful, and very different day, in His presence, as it was now quite late, and I could do with something to eat!

Like a heavy weight on my shoulders, I heard the Almighty say, "Wait! This is only the first half, the second half of the story is still to be told! Make yourself comfortable, there is a lot more to come."

"Please Lord," I pleaded, "no more hardships and misery! The first half was more than I could bear!" The Lord said nothing, and I continued sitting and praying!

Jan Van Wyk, Sarel junior's son, had just turned 33 when the first democratic election took place in April 1994. Jan and his wife, Poppy (her nickname), had been married for 11 years and had given 'Oupagrootjie'[140] Sarel two delightful grandchildren, Theunis and Sonja.

Both children were at a Model C school and often told stories of their school friends, many of whom had Black names, but this didn't worry the two of them. However, Oupagrootjie Sarel and Oupa Sarel were not very impressed. But for the sake

---

[140] Afrikaans for 'Great-grandfather'.

of the children, and the new political dispensation, they made no comment, at least not until they were asleep.

Sarel senior still enjoyed his brandy and coke at his ripe old age, and often would comment, *"Dis 'n skande!"*[141]

"Los dit, asseblief, pa!"[142] was Sarel junior's reply.

But this new mixed schooling arrangement was too much for the old man, and Sarel junior had also had enough. It appeared to him that the Blacks were simply taking over, and he often wondered how long his police pension would remain in place. He had heard from younger policemen that promotions for Whites had been halted, and any advancement for Whites in the police force was improbable.

Sarel junior was privately pleased that Jan had employment at the Johannesburg Municipality's electrical department and that there didn't seem to be the same political bias as there was in the police force. He was also glad that his son and daughter-in-law had the use of a council house at a reduced rental.

A full year passed when Sarel senior fell ill, and because he was on a railway pension, the family had to take him to the nearest provincial hospital. The Joburg Gen, in its day, had been one of the top teaching hospitals in the country, second only to Groote Schuur in Cape Town. The building was clean, and the treatment was good and professional.

However, when Sarel was admitted, the family were surprised to hear that they had to bring their own bedding and a pillow for their Oupagrootjie. Sarel junior rushed back to the house and collected what was needed, thinking to himself that this was very unusual. Once back at the hospital, he found the old man and his family still sitting where he had left them,

---

[141] Afrikaans for 'It's a scandal!'

[142] Afrikaans for 'Leave it, please, Dad!'

waiting to be assigned a bed, and no doctor had seen him yet. After numerous enquiries, Sarel stopped asking and joined the rest of the anxious family.

It took a further three hours of waiting, in a congested waiting area, before a very disinterested nurse asked the family to follow her to the third floor. They had to walk up three flights of stairs because "The lift is broken," the nurse told them.

Fortunately, Sarel junior and Jan were strong men, and almost carried the old man up the stairs.

On reaching the third floor, they waited while the nurse who accompanied them had a heated discussion with the sister in charge, and eventually, a bed was assigned with only a mattress. No one offered to make the bed, so Poppy and Jan used the bedding from home, to make up the bed. A very tired, Sarel senior climbed into bed. The family saw just how full the ward was, and they didn't think that any one of the other patients could speak their father's language!

It was nearly midnight when a doctor approached the bed. His accent showed that he was from Nigeria, and he was only able to speak English. After examining the old man, he turned to Sarel junior.

"What is wrong with my father?"

"I cannot say until we have conducted more tests," came the reply from an obviously overworked doctor.

"When will you be able to conduct these tests?" Sarel tried to keep his cool.

"In the morning."

And with that, he left the bewildered family.

They made Oupa comfortable, and left the hospital, telling him that they would see him the next day. They noted how tired their father was. It was now after midnight, and as he made his way to the car, Sarel wondered how the mighty Joburg Gen had sunk so low, after only a few years of the new government coming into office. With this thought, he drove the family home.

Sadly, two days later, Sarel senior passed away peacefully, in his sleep. The hospital gave the reason for death as multiple organ failure. Sarel senior, the patriarch of the Van Wyk family, was buried at West Park Cemetery. The memorial service reminded Sarel junior of the one he had attended in Van Stadensrus, when his uncle Piet had been buried, after being murdered on his farm, by unknown gunmen. The perpetrators had taken firearms and the farm bakkie (pick-up truck), and until this day, the crime had not been solved, even though many strings had been pulled through contacts in the police force.

Just two months after Sarel's funeral, the spotlight fell on Jan and Poppy. Jan was at work, as usual on Monday morning when he and some of his colleagues were called into the Head of Department's office.

"Close the door please," said Mr Cilliers. This was not a usual practice when speaking to his staff. He cleared his throat and faced the men before him. "The new bosses at the council have informed me that each of you has to reapply for your present position in the department."

Everyone, present in the room, knew that some ANC members had just received top positions in the electrical department, even though they had no electrical training whatsoever!

"Wat?"[143] came the chorus.

"Ek het vir amper twintig jaar hier gewerk!"[144] exploded

---

[143] Afrikaans for 'What?'
[144] Afrikaans for 'I have worked here for almost twenty years!'

Jan. "Hoekom moet ek nou annsoek doen vir my eie pos?"[145]

"I don't know. I also have to apply for my position, which I have held for almost forty years!" said a dejected and confused Cilliers. "If we don't apply, they have said that we will be put on early retirement."

There was a deathly hush in the room. Everyone there knew the reason for this. The ANC government had made it clear that Black people were to be employed in government and semi-governmental institutions. No one in the room spoke. They all knew what this early retirement meant! It was another way of forced retrenchment of White staff.

Cilliers concluded the meeting by saying, "Please take an application form, fill it out, and return it by Wednesday." They all took forms and applied for their positions, all except Cilliers, who applied for early retirement. They all needed their jobs and were the backbone of the electrical department with their years of training and experience. The infrastructure of the city relied on their knowledge and expertise.

The applications were adjudicated. Everyone, except for Elizabeth Jones, a cripple in the accounts department, and Javid, an Indian technician, lost their jobs, and were officially retrenched.

It was a very dejected Jan who returned home that day, with just a cardboard box containing things he had on his desk for the last twenty-odd years!

---

[145] Afrikaans for 'Why do I now have to apply for my own job?'

Chapter 26

"So, what now, Almighty God?" I asked. Then, as if in a flash, I saw a vision of a deer giving birth to a foal. The vision immediately reminded me how many times I had seen the birth of a foal on the nature channel, or the wildlife programme on TV. Here was the mother doe, alone in a slightly wooded, but grassy area, giving birth to her baby. Her back arches for a moment; then the miracle - a sack, containing the foal, drops to the ground. As it does, it bursts open, freeing the baby, and ridding the sack of the protective waters that kept the baby safe while in the womb.

The clock starts ticking, and the background music on the television audio starts to gain volume and momentum.

Come on, I say to myself. Stand up! But the foal's legs are still very new, and cannot take the weight of its body yet!

The doe turns around, with her ears turned back, listening for sounds of danger. She approaches her baby and starts to lick it, and for a moment time stands still! The foal manages to get up onto its front legs, and they wobble and crumble. "Please get up!" I shout at the television screen. The foal tries again; first the front legs and then success! It manages to get the back legs up, and on four wobbly legs, it finds its mother. The two unite and the immediate danger has passed!

Khazimela and his wife, Akhona, had rented a two-bedroomed house in the suburb of Dobsonville in Soweto, with the view of getting better accommodation later. After all, the cadres had been promised great wealth while they were still in the camps outside the borders of South Africa. This fortune was not precisely described by the expectations of the returning cadres, but they were indeed high!

Khazimela was well into his sixties at the time, and although he had an original degree in political science, this degree, in post-apartheid South Africa, was worthless. He had absolutely no commercial work experience and had no idea how he was going to earn a living. He held on to the promise of great wealth.

A short while later, he got a call from his family in Kagwana, telling him that his father, Fundile, head of the Khumalo family, had passed on to be with his ancestors. Khazimela and Akhona hastily packed some clothes into two suitcases, and headed for the major taxi rank near the massive Baragwanath Hospital, internationally recognised as one of the finest academic hospitals in Africa, especially in the treatment of burn wounds.

At the rank, they made their way to the vehicles used for 'long distance' and found the one going to King Williamstown, in the Eastern Cape. Once there, they would get another one to take them to the homestead. They could have taken a train, which at that time, was efficient and a lot safer, but speed was of the essence.

They negotiated a price for their fare plus luggage, and paid the driver, before boarding the Toyota mini-bus taxi. Taxis operated on a system that as soon as it was full, it would leave the taxi rank. But in this case, there were still two empty seats, and it was a case of waiting patiently for two more passengers to arrive. It could take five minutes or two hours, no one ever knew!

Fortunately, after about twenty-minutes a family of four arrived, parents with two teenage children. The fact that there were only two seats available didn't faze the driver one bit! Everyone just had to move up to make room for the extra two people. It was extremely uncomfortable, but unless you wanted to wait for another ride, you had to keep your mouth closed! Khazimela had to get to his father's house as soon as he could, so he kept quiet.

Exactly eleven hours, with three stops en-route, the overloaded taxi pulled into the rank at King Williamstown. The next ride to the family homestead was much more pleasurable, and even though the road was full of potholes and was bumpy, it was a relief from their former journey. Khazimela made a note to be sure to catch the train home after the funeral.

It was about midday when they walked up the path to the kraal and main homestead area. The dogs barked at them as they approached with their suitcases, and as they entered the house, they could immediately sense the mood of extreme sadness and loss. Fundile had been a great father, and although his income had been meagre, he had always sent money home, and with the proceeds of his cattle and goats, the family had lived reasonable lives. They had managed to put their children through an education system that had been rudimentary in the extreme.

Khazimela, being the oldest of the twins, and the son, immediately involved himself with the finer details of the funeral arrangements, even though the rest of the family had started preparations anyway. In this, and similar households, detail and adherence to traditions, were very important.

The day of the funeral arrived, and members of their

extended family, and friends, arrived at the kraal to pay their respects. It was custom that catering was done well, and a bull was slaughtered for the occasion. All ancestral rites were carefully observed, and Fundile was finally laid to rest at the base of the family tree, near the entrance to the kraal. He had died an honest man, certainly not ranked a wealthy man, but a man of dignity, who had grown up under the apartheid system, and had managed to steer his life, and that of his family, through it all. Now he was laid to rest, and hopefully, his children and grandchildren would at least reap the profit of his patience.

A few days later, and after a more comfortable train trip back to Johannesburg, Khazimela and Akhona arrived at their home in Dobsonville. It was now time for Khazimela to find a well-paying job. He didn't have to wait very long!

In terms of the new political dispensation, and what was becoming the order of the day, all companies listed on the JSE were required to forfeit a portion of their equity to persons of colour. If they were a non-listed company, it was necessary, and politically correct, for them to hand out directorships to persons of colour. This arrangement was passed into law, under what was loosely labelled Black Economic Empowerment (BEE). Non-compliance would mean that such companies would no longer have access to government or provincial tenders and contracts. This was one way of ensuring, a more representative work and managerial staff. Although not clearly defined, companies were expected to give up a majority shareholding to persons of colour.

In principle, this new ownership-equity programme was not a bad idea and would open doors for the previously disadvantaged people to have access to better work opportunities and a share of the nation's collective wealth. In essence, it was a complete recipe for corruption. The system was manipulated in every possible way, from the so-called persons of colour, the previously disadvantaged people, to the companies and organisations themselves!

The reasons were basic. Firstly, the majority of persons of colour did not have the commercial knowledge or background qualifications, to offer any real financial support to the companies, that now had to employ new staff! With the exception of those exiled outside the country, particularly in Europe and Asia, commercial knowledge was sparse, and the reservoir of expertise was therefore generally empty.

Secondly, the reason was even more basic, and this was the companies themselves. In their struggle to comply with the new legislation and become the new buzz words, 'BEE Compliant', they were employing people of colour, even though they were not qualified to hold these new positions, now thrust on them by listed and otherwise constituted companies.

The awful result of both these factors, save for a few qualified individuals, was that unqualified and inexperienced people were taking up positions in the commercial and business fields. This was evident in local city and town councils that had been taken over by the ANC during local elections.

Knowing the right person, or being at the right place at the right time, was the order of the day. And if you had served the cause during the fight for freedom, then you automatically qualified for a position with any company that needed to fulfil its BEE quota. Qualifications were not a top priority. So, it wasn't surprising for Khazimela to be summoned to an *uMkhonto we Sizwe* veteran's meeting, and to be handed a list of three companies that had positions available on their boards of directors.

It was simple enough. Khazimela made arrangements for an interview with two of the companies of his choice and was offered a seat on the board, and shares, which he could 'earn' over the next few months. The one company, a listed company, offered to make him a shareholder, and director of human sustainability, and the other, an unlisted one, offered him a shareholding and a directorship of company assets. He had no idea what these job descriptions and titles meant, and neither did either of the companies concerned. But it didn't matter. From being a guerrilla fighter to being a company director, in a few short years, was absolutely perfect, and he decided on the listed company.

He took up his seat on the board, and received a six-digit annual salary, plus director's fees, together with a car of his choice. It was time for the family to move from Dobsonville, in Soweto, to a newly developed cluster unit in the leafy suburb of Oaklands, in the northern suburbs of Johannesburg.

The listed company soon displayed the company title to state BEE approved, and no one cared.

Chapter 27

I had got so caught up with the foal getting up on to its feet, and safely running off into the thicket that I hadn't noticed the shadows, due to the sun now shining in through the west window, and casting a totally different shadow across the church transept, either side of the altar.

But it was the right transept that caught my attention. A very dark shadow had been appearing the whole time I had been sitting in the pew. The shadow dominated the west nave, and the shadow on the transept was starting to lift.

I was fascinated. I hadn't realised until this moment, how this original shadow was so dominant and almost overbearing, and that it was the reason that the building was so dark, save for the odd ray of sunshine during the first morning hours!

The more I looked at the shadow, the more I longed for it to lift. Eventually, it did, a little with each ray of light from the afternoon sun.

What a massive relief! This shadow had been chased away by the piercing rays of the afternoon sun, which was now shining through the western windows. Like a miracle, the dark shadow on the right had lifted and gone! There was at last light, and the whole church building took on a new hue.

It struck me that from this display of shapes and shadows, I had learnt a new lesson. And it was a simple one – "Don't let a shadow blur your thinking; there is a new light that will rise!" Just for a moment, I smiled, "This is what it is all about," I said to myself.

And then I looked again. "No! It's not possible!" I shouted out loud. But it was not only possible, it was happening. The shadow had crossed from the right side of the transept, and was now clearly forming its ugliness on the left side of the transept; the church was again fading into darkness.

The indices on the stock exchange that were displayed on television at the end of the nightly news, looked promising. The JSE was having a bull run after so many years of uncertainty and the biting edge of International sanctions. It was now gaining momentum; each news report showed a rise in the overall share index, and at last, the Reserve Bank was bringing down its prime lending rate.

Overseas investors and lenders were knocking at the door of South Africa's industry. A new age had dawned, and most of the English-speaking population were saying to themselves, "We told this to the National Party, years ago," while silently hoping that their White status and income wouldn't be affected, should the Blacks come into power.

Sadly, Michael John died peacefully in his sleep the following January, but he had led a full life and, thankfully, a healthy one. All through his working career, he had been diligent with his money, and during the thirty years he had been living off his bank pension, he had been living well. He often joked with his family that the bank pension scheme had paid his pension for nearly the same time that he had worked for the bank! And so, upon Michael John's death, the Porter-Smith family closed a dear chapter in their lives.

Six months later, David was retrenched as a result of his company making a very stupid business mistake, which put the company into liquidation, and David found himself out of work. The irony was that the country was on its way to financial recovery, so it was reasonable to think that new employment would be easily obtainable. But as a White male, doors to new employment were nil, and this was the beginning of reverse apartheid!

If you were Black, the doors were immediately opened to you, and if you were a woman, your chances were enhanced. However, if you were disabled then your chances were excellent! The saying went around that if you were a 'pale' male, don't even bother to apply for corporate, government, or semi-government work. If, however, fortune smiled on you, you might be placed in a government-controlled enterprise as a 'token' White in some obscure position. This had to be done to ensure that the company could prove that they were not completely racially biased.

A second notion doing the rounds was if you were a Black, disabled woman, you were easily going to get the top-rated jobs in the country, even if you were not trained for that position. The apartheid wheel was starting to turn full circle, and instead of it being dead and buried with the 1994 election, the ghost of apartheid was rising... but now the shoe was on the other foot!

After numerous attempts and many disappointments, David became bitter and disillusioned with what everyone in the world called 'the new South Africa'. There was only one option left for him and that was to go it alone! So, he took the plunge and opened his own company, doing exactly what he had been doing for years. Only, this time David was responsible for his future, and his paycheque!

In the meantime, David's daughter, Paula, had finished her third year at a private university and had qualified with a

Bachelor of Commerce degree, specialising in human resources. David realised from his own experience that in the new political dispensation, it was imperative to have some form of tertiary education because an ordinary matric would not open any doors. He made a mental note to ensure that the application for his son, Sean, was in for the first semester at the same university for the following year.

David's new company was quickly formed, and he was blessed with work almost immediately. He got all the latest tools of the trade, personal computer and the likes, and signed up two additional staff members who would join him in this venture. He learnt that he should not employ the staff in the old-fashioned way when they were put on the company monthly payroll. Instead, it was better to employ them on a contract basis, whereby they would pass the company an invoice for work done at an agreed hourly rate.

This had massive advantages, in that the company did not have to fulfil any BEE requirements, and his company qualified as a one-man business, again not being subjected to BEE criteria! Also, as the staff were not formally employed, he did not have to deal with the unions in that particular industry.

The unions were a real threat to the economy because they were figuratively in bed with the government, and the government was thus forced to kowtow to the wishes of the unions. Gone were the days when an employer could simply say, "You're fired!"

That was history, and time would show that employees could both wreck the company and the economy simply because an employee couldn't be dismissed from their post.

David reckoned that he had made the right decision, and he remembered that his dad had once said, "Money talks!"

This saying was going to be the only safe guard that Whites would hold on to as the dragnet of reverse apartheid and unionism took a firm grip on South Africa, the people, and the economy.

As time went by, Paula started her search for employment. With the help of a professional, she put together her Curriculum Vitae (CV) and had it nicely printed and bound. She found almost fifty companies that were looking to hire BCom graduates – exactly the qualification she had. She carefully addressed the CVs to the Human Resource Officer of each of these companies and posted her CV's to them. She felt sure that one of the companies was sure to offer her a position, but all the answers came back negative because as a White female, she did not fit the BEE status of the companies concerned!

However, one CV that did come back reasonably positive, was from an American Company with a huge franchise footprint throughout South Africa. The reply simply stated, "Kindly make an appointment to see our Human Resources (HR) manager." She did just that, and the HR manager was a White South African male; she got the post and could start immediately.

Sean was enrolled at the same university that his sister had recently graduated from, but his course was for a bachelor's degree that would give him a British qualification in business administration.

And so, the Porter-Smith family were embarking on a new business, a new career and a new course of study. Meanwhile, David's wife Sarah-Jean, who had dedicated her entire working life to education, found herself in an extremely strange situation. With the opening of all government schools, typically the original 'Model C' schools, to all races, Black parents clamoured for places for their children at predominately White suburban schools. The result was that class numbers rose from twenty-five to forty or more!

These suburban schools catered for a specific feeder area, normally for immediate suburbs around the school, but the new dispensation stated that if a parent worked in that area of influence, then the child was entitled to attend that school. This theory only worked on paper! Parents, desperately wanting to give their children a better education, cheated in every possible way to falsify residential addresses, so that their child would gain admission to that particular school. An avalanche of applications was received, many fraudulent, and many cases of threats and intimidation were launched at the schools which turned down the false ones.

The result was inevitable. Model C schools were inundated with pupils of colour, and many White children, whose parents could afford private education, left. Within a single year, privately run schools emerged throughout the country, and educational apartheid took hold. The irony was that White teachers remained the top choice of educators, for the children of other races.

Verbal abuse, a lack of genuine support from education authorities and parents, and a lack of commitment to school work by learners, soon took their toll. Many teachers with decades of experience left the government system in favour of positions offered at private schools. Parents were allowed to apply for a grant to pay for their child's education, and this placed a burden on schools that relied on the fees to cover running costs. Education levels dropped, the pass rate kept being lowered to accommodate a false level of achievement, and within a few short years, South African government education dropped to one of the lowest in the world. Maths and Science subjects were the hardest hit!

The government would not listen to educators who had years of experience. The pass rate was dropped to 35% and in a lot of schools the call for "Pass one! Pass all!" became the rallying call of the badly educated masses.

Chapter 28

I heard myself say, "Lord, how can this happen again? How can the darkness that was so awful, simply change sides?"

I paused to listen for an answer, but nothing audible came. However, if this particular morning had taught me anything, it was that I should be patient, and wait for the light on the panes to keep changing, and for little visions to come to me.

I didn't have to wait long. Several tiny insects, little bugs and moths, had been exposed briefly by the light, as the shadow changed sides from the right to the left of the transept. Now, this group was clearly exposed, and their hiding places were revealed for all to see. All, was just me and a grey gecko that had now taken up a threatening position, waiting to swoop on anyone of these tiny creatures.

And this is exactly what the gecko did! With impeccable timing, and without regard for life or limb, he quickly gobbled up moth after moth!

This was quite clearly the gecko's turn, and he was going to make the most of this exquisite buffet!

Theunis and Sonja, Jan Van Wyk's children, arrived home from school on the day that Jan had lost his job. This was due to the reshuffling of the workforce at the city's electrical department.

Sarel junior was sitting in his armchair listening to an old long-playing vinyl record, on his equally old turn table. He had not got into the more modern CDs which were now on the market. He immediately noticed the dejected expression on his son, Jan's face, and asked, "Wat pla my seun?"[146]

"Ek het my werk verloor,"[147] came the reply. "Ek het amper twintig jare van my lewe opgeoffer vir die council, en nou is ek nie genoeg nie!"[148]

"Wat bedoel jy?"[149]

"Hulle gaan my werk vir 'n swarte gee, en ek is nou sonder werk."[150]

Before Sarel junior could comment, Jan turned his back and stomped out of the room. Jan and Poppie were destroyed. They certainly weren't wealthy people by any stretch of the imagination, and they relied completely on Jan's salary each month to put food on the table, pay the rent and pay the fees at the school that the children attended. Sarel junior did help a little by paying his police pension into the general household fund each month.

Fortunately, Theunis only had a year to finish his schooling, and Sonja had one more. They were both average learners and passed the final exams each year with above-average marks, but certainly not enough for them to qualify to go to university. Theunis had already said that he wanted to go to the Technical College and study to become an electrician like his dad! This pleased Jan.

But the family had little or nothing in the way of savings, so it was imperative that Jan find new employment

---

[146] Afrikaans for 'What is worrying you, son?'
[147] Afrikaans for 'I lost my job'.
[148] Afrikaans for 'I have given almost twenty years to the council and now I'm not good enough!'
[149] Afrikaans for 'What do you mean?'
[150] Afrikaans for 'They are giving my job to a Black, and now I am out of work'.

immediately. It was little relief knowing that Jan would receive a small severance package from the council, made up of outstanding leave pay and his portion of the pension fund. But this could take months to be finalised and paid out, so Jan bought the newspaper every day and scoured the 'employment vacancies' column, but there was nothing. He was forty years old, and a White male, so that disqualified him from 90% of the jobs advertised.

Days turned into weeks and still nothing worthwhile; disillusionment set in. Jan became impatient and depressed, questioning every motive of his family. His father complained that he was drinking and smoking too much, which led to an almighty row, culminating in Sonja slamming the door as she left the house, to go and stay with a friend.

Poppie did what she could, and even started baking for the local 'tuisnywerheid',[151] to keep the wolf from the door.

Calls to the council to follow up on Jan's payout continued without much success, and all the while Jan was slipping more and more into a deep depression. In his mind, he still had a good pair of hands and a good mind to do work and earn an honest living, but the new BEE system was really taking its toll.

"Wat het ek gedoen? Hoekom haat hulle ons so?"[152] he asked his father. "Ek het niks slegs gedoen! Maar ek is 'n wit man, en nou kry ek geen werk nie!"[153] Jan's depression grew and grew, and eventually, he stopped buying the newspaper. It was by chance, that one day he was talking to his neighbour across the fence when the neighbour asked if Jan had applied

---

[151] Afrikaans for 'home industries'.

[152] Afrikaans for 'What have I done? Why do they hate us so?'

[153] Afrikaans for 'I have done nothing wrong! But I am a White man and now I can get no work.'

for a monthly payment from the Unemployment Insurance Fund (UIF).

Jan had never given it a thought!

"Get your last payslip," instructed the neighbour, and waited while Jan went to fetch it. "There it is!" said the neighbour pointing to an amount on the payslip. "You have been paying UIF for months. You need to go and apply for what is owed to you."

Early the next morning, Jan joined the queue of many unemployed workers at the UIF office. He looked up and down the row. There were people of all colours, but he noticed how many White middle-aged men and women were standing in the line! How had his life come to this, thought Jan dozens of times that day, as he waited in line to fill out the forms. Fortunately, it was relatively simple to complete the form, and when he handed it back, he was told that he could collect the first of six payments the following Tuesday. He thanked the clerk and left, but instead of exiting the building the way he had entered, he accidentally found himself in the SASSA offices. (South African Social Services Authority.)

An official asked Jan if he could help him, and Jan asked what was done in these offices, to which it was explained that he could get a government grant paid out each month if he applied and met the criteria. The official jokingly asked if Jan was pregnant because he could then qualify for a child grant! He didn't fit any of the criteria, so he made his way home where he was greeted by an elated Poppie, who told him that his severance package cheque had been delivered. Jan opened the envelope and saw that the amount was more generous than expected, but this didn't stop him from feeling how much he missed his normal working day!

That night the family gathered after supper to discuss a way forward. Jan had spent two hours by himself before dinner, thinking about what they should do with the money. Sarel junior poured himself a large dop, and Theunis and Sonja were invited to participate in the discussion.

No one knew what the meeting was about, but they all knew that it was serious, so they paid attention.

Jan began by explaining that he had lost his job due to the new BEE status in the council, and he lamented how hard it was for him not to be able to go to work. He told them all that he wasn't sure how the family would survive, and then went on to regale everyone with stories about the good old days before the 1994 elections. Finally, he said, "Ek het besluit om my eie elektriese besigheid te begin."[154]

The family said nothing but looked at one another too scared to speak. At last, Sarel junior spoke up, "Dis 'n goeie idee my seun, sterkte!"[155] Jan was delighted with this response and went on to explain that he would get a second-hand bakkie[156] and all the electrical tools he needed, besides the ones he had in the garage. Thankfully, his electrical operator's licence was still valid, and he asked Poppie to please look it out in the morning.

"Pa, waar gaan jy werk kry?"[157] asked Sonja. Jan explained that he would have posters printed and some flyers, and would ask local businesses to please put up the posters and hand out the flyers. He would also ask the minister at their church whether he could place an advert in the church newsletter.

---

[154] Afrikaans for 'I have decided to start my own electrical business'.
[155] Afrikaans for 'It's a good idea, son. Strength!'
[156] Afrikaans for 'small pick-up truck'.
[157] Afrikaans for 'Dad, where will you get work?'

As far as he was concerned, the meeting was over, and he wished them all a good night and went to his room and closed the door. Jan's Electrical Contracting Company had just been formed!

Chapter 29

I felt sick to my stomach, watching that gecko eating those moths and bugs. He didn't discriminate. He had only one purpose in mind, and that was to eat as much as he could, while the harvest, so to speak, was abundant!

As I watched this unfold, out of the shadows yet another gecko appeared. This fellow was twice the size of the first, who by now could hardly eat another thing. Slowly, and sure-footedly, the second gecko got closer, but the smaller one stood his ground for a while and then decided that it was not worth a probable fight, with an opponent nearly twice his size. So, having had his fill, he moved off, leaving the large one to carry on feeding. After all, there was enough for everyone.

Again, a massacre of bugs and moths, and there was little regard shown for dining etiquette, or for at least allowing the younger bugs to get away! No, just eating, eating, eating! It was what geckos do, but it was still awful.

Khazimela, Akhona and their children, Bongani and Babalwa, settled nicely into their home in the suburb of Oaklands. They were not surprised to find that their neighbours on the left were White, those behind were also White, but on the right was an Indian family. The Indian neighbour was a businessman, originally from Tongaat in KwaZulu-Natal and he drove a flashy BMW, an X3. Each time he came home, he would call to Khazimela over the fence and start up a conversation, calling

Khazimela "My Bru!"

Khazimela hated this and did everything possible to avoid his neighbour, but the car intrigued him. So, at the next company board meeting, he surprised his fellow board members by stating that he required a better vehicle than the Audi 6 that he had been given. Khazimela actually could add nothing of substance to the running of the enterprise, but he knew that they could not afford to lose their BEE status.

Some of the board members raised their eyebrows. After all, he had been given one of the top vehicles in the company fleet. After a while, the director of human resources said, "I dare say we can look into this matter. What vehicle did you have in mind, Mr Khumalo?"

"I rather like the 500 X class Mercedes Benz," he answered. This made the board members sit up and look at one another. None of them had cars of this stature, so they looked at the chairman for guidance. He usually answered questions and made quick decisions, but today he leant across and whispered something to the CFO. Was the BEE status so important that it warranted the leasing of a new Mercedes Benz for someone who had added nothing to the company over the last few months?

The CFO whispered something back to the chairman, who was the founder and owner of the company. He cleared his throat and said, "Will the director of human resources attend to this matter as one of urgency, and instruct the fleet manager to lease a 500 X class Mercedes Benz for Mr Khumalo."

A pin could be dropped in that room, such was the silence, as each person looked at the other in absolute amazement. Was this the start, the small edge of the wedge, being driven into a company that had been trading for nearly eighty years?

Three days later, Khazimela drove into his driveway and parked his brand-new car where his Indian neighbour could see it. Neighbours to the left and the back just drew their curtains and continued preparing the evening meal. This was another story they could tell their friends around the next braai.

In the meantime, Akhona was doing particularly well, and taking full advantage of the new economic fortune that was feeding the previously disadvantaged, especially those associated with the new ruling party. She had given up her work at the retirement home and had joined her brother, Elias, in the construction of Reconstruction and Development Programme (RDP) housing. The programme had been launched by the government to cater for the massive backlog in affordable housing for families with a combined income of R3,500.00 per month. At first, a unit of two rooms was built, but later as time went by, five-roomed houses became more acceptable.

The building of these RDP houses fell under the auspices of the Department of Human Resources and the control of the Government Housing Department. As far as the government was concerned, this initiative was given much support and was seen as a constructive step in assisting the otherwise marginalised population. Billions of rands were pumped into the collective effort. But it would not escape corruption, and so poor construction methods were used, and the initiative was lauded as a great step forward in giving a family a place they could truly call home!

Elias was another political appointee into the Department of Human Resources, and through the chairman, he was given access to the tender department who controlled the awarding of tenders to approved companies in the construction of RDP houses throughout the country. So, it wasn't by chance, or without planning, that Akhona started a construction company, specializing in the building of RDP houses. The first thing she did was rent a small office in a Sandton office block. She placed a desk and chair in the office, signed up with a telephone provider, and put a sign on her door – A. Khumalo & Sons, Construction Company cc. She then had some letterheads printed, bought a cheap PC and printer from the pawn shop, and was now in the construction business, and ready to roll out one of many RDP houses.

In no time, the notice to tender on batches of a hundred and two hundred houses being built all over the country, accumulated on her desk. She immediately phoned Elias, as she didn't have a clue, not the foggiest notion. She had no construction knowledge, to even be able to price one house, let alone a hundred, and all the related infrastructure.

"Relax," he advised. "Just choose one contract not far from your home, say in Diepsloot. I sent you that tender document yesterday."

"Yebo, I have it," she said after a break in the conversation.

"Count up the number of houses in the contract, and multiply by..." He gave her a figure. "Now that is what you put on the tender document. Fill in the details and hand the tender into the department."

"But how do we know what the tender amount is?" she enquired.

"It doesn't matter. I will sort out the details," he assured her. "Just fill in the tender."

Akhona did the calculation and arrived at a figure well over fifteen million, and she wrote it into the tender document. She filled in all her details and then delivered the document to the tender board. The official at the desk gave her a receipt and informed her that the tender would be opened the next morning at ten sharp and that she was allowed to be present at the opening of the tenders. She had no idea what to expect but said that she would attend the next day. She left the building.

That night she phoned her brother and told him that he was allowed to be at the tender openings in the morning. "Good," he said. "Now listen carefully, and write down the name of the company that offers the lowest price for the work, and get their details. Do you understand?"

"Yes, but what about my tender?"

"Don't worry about that for now. That will all come later. Just do as I say." Elias ended the call.

The next day Akhona made her way to the tender openings. She wasn't the first there either. She took a seat and looked around. There were numerous people, of all races, sitting waiting, each with a copy of their tender document in their hand. Most of them were men, but she did notice one other woman on the far side of the room.

She listened to the conversations going on around her. The common thread in the conversations was the building industry, and many of the people seemed to know one another. Akhona was completely out of her depth, and she prayed that no one would ask her a question.

Eventually, an officer came into the room with a pile of unopened envelopes. He wished everyone a good morning, and Akhona noticed that he was wearing a ruling party T-shirt. He announced that he represented the tender committee of the Department of Human Resources, and then went on to read out the number of the contract and the area where the work was to be done.

The silence was palpable as the first envelope was opened. The document was taken out, the tender value was called out, first in figures, and then in words. Akhona was disappointed to hear that the price was over a million less than her price. The second envelope revealed a price very close to hers. Eventually, all the tenders had been revealed, and it was plain to see that J.C. Van Staden Builders had offered the lowest price of just over twelve million for the completion of the entire project.

A middle-aged man, obviously Mr Van Staden, got up and shouted "Great!" and then sat down again. There were many words of congratulations passed around the room, and the unsuccessful applicants left the room one by one. As Elias had instructed, Akhona waited for her chance and then made her way over to the gentleman who had won the tender. He was still sitting, but as he got up, she interrupted him.

"Excuse me, sir. Are you from Van Staden's Builders?"

"Yes, I am the owner. How can I help you?"

"I am Akhona. Please tell me how long it will take for the contracts to be finally awarded?"

"Pleased to meet you, Akhona. It usually takes about two weeks for the department to check through the applications, and then for them to check on the credibility of the contractors. Why do you ask?"

"I am just interested. Do you have a business card, Mr Van Staden?" He reached into his pocket and handed her the card. She thanked him, and they both left.

She was hardly back at her office when the phone rang. It was Elias, but before he could speak, she asked him why he had over-quoted on the tender.

"Wait a minute! Did you get the details of the company that was awarded the tender?" She told him who it was, and he replied, "I know them. Relax, I will phone you in a few days," and the line went dead.

The Tender Department adjudicated the tenders, and Van Stadens were the legitimate winners because they had offered the lowest price. Their credentials were thoroughly checked, and everything, except for one, was in order. Their company had only a level 2 Black Empowerment rating, whereas Akhona's company had a level 3 rating, even though her bid was the highest!

This was indeed a problem for Van Staden, but not for the skilled Elias, who had valuable contacts in the Department for RDP housing. He moved quickly and phoned Van Staden, and set up a private meeting with him for late that evening.

The plan was simple. Elias would explain that their tender was indeed the lowest, but that they lacked the necessary BEE rating. However, he knew of a company that had the right rating and did qualify on these grounds. So, Elias would have the tender awarded to the qualified BEE company, which in turn would employ Van Staden's Builders to do the work at their original price, and the BEE company would pay them directly.

It was a win-win situation. Akhona would get the contract at R15 million, and Van Staden would be paid his original bid of just over R12 million! Van Staden's company would do the work, and Akhona would sit back and reap the profits! It was just another day in the tender department.

Chapter 30

The old-fashioned clock on the back wall was now showing that it was close to four o'clock, and I decided that it was time to take my leave and find my way home.

This had been a day of many revelations, some chatting with my Maker but so many unresolved questions remained.

I had seen hope; I had seen fear; I had seen cruelty; I had seen the ghost of dark shadows; I had seen absolute beauty, and I had witnessed joy and encouragement!

As I summed up the day, I was suddenly filled with despair, and I began to cry. I suddenly remembered the great author, Alan Paton, who had written that memorable book, 'Cry the Beloved Country' – a book that had gained him fame and recognition.

"Alan, I don't know what your motive was, when you wrote that book, but let me tell you something, nothing has really changed. There is still distrust, envy and greed in the country that we call our own! People are still cheating. People are still leaving their homes for what would appear to be greener pastures because they have been denied a better future!"

The only difference is that the shadow, the dark shadow, has come full circle, and instead of us learning from our mistakes, we have now turned from being the hunted into the hunter.

By now the tears were running unashamedly down my face, and my mouth and throat felt bitter as I tried to swallow. These tears, dear reader, are for the country that I call home.

I left the little place of worship, carefully closing the door behind me. The sun was just about to set.

David's business grew in leaps and bounds. This was mainly due to the adage of 'The old school tie!' This simply meant that those who had a similar upbringing and shared the same values, would keep their businesses 'in-house' so to speak.

With this thought in mind, and because it was virtually impossible to get work without being BEE-connected, government, provincial and municipal work was unavailable. But there was work available through the 'old school tie' system. And, so, the gulf between private and government work became more and more apparent.

The failure of government contracts would arise from the widespread corruption that soon started to take root in what would be the so-called formal sector. State Owned Enterprises (SOEs) like the Electricity Supply Commission (Eskom), the original railway network (PRASA), South African Airways (SAA), and others soon found massive cracks in their systems, particularly in their finances. Dodgy deals, the awarding of suspect tenders to friends of the ruling party, became major contributors to the quick slide into a quagmire of failure and disillusionment. And to think that these SOEs and municipalities had been robust, profitable enterprises just a few short years before!

Corruption and labour unions, as well as unskilled staff, all added to the burden of failure. Every ensuing national budget became burdened with bailouts to be paid to failing SOEs. At the same time, the public called for the sale of these SOEs to private businesses. This would involve trimming down a bulging and unnecessary staff wage bill, but it would be the saving of all these enterprises. Nobody would listen!

In the meantime, a new phrase was being bandied about, 'White monopoly capital'. This was the result of the 'old school tie' sticking together, developing businesses and private infrastructure, and utilizing the most valuable resource of all, the skills of the people, regardless of colour or creed!

But the 'capital' stayed inhouse and the anonymity kept growing. Failing government enterprises on the one side, and private, White monopoly capital on the other. The brightness of the Rainbow Nation was starting to fade. The euphoria of the Mandela era dissipated, and President Mandela wasn't able to fill the head of government post for the next term.

His replacement, Thabo Mbeki, was seen by all to be a good leader, and the economy responded favourably to his appointment. It did seem that there was a chance for this magnificent country. But the Mbeki era was soon shattered when a faction of the ANC did not approve of his governing skills, and he was 'recalled', making way for Jacob Zuma. This beautiful country was in for an almighty fall!

Corruption and maladministration were the order of the day. 'Money for chommies' would become the catchphrase, and the poor would get poorer, and the rich, richer. This was a stark reality!

The complete essence of the struggle against apartheid was to put people on an equal footing, and to ensure that everyone, regardless of colour or creed, would enjoy the wealth of the land; everyone would have equal rights to work, wealth, land and homes. Hundreds had died for these principles, but the new government had very different thoughts, and simply bled the economy into their pockets, bypassing the masses of poor and vulnerable people.

Soon, overseas rating agencies started downgrading the country's future outlook for investments, and the proverbial fat cow, because it was being looted and no longer fed properly, simply stopped its milk supply!

David's business ticked on, as did many others, and the commercial market continued providing. White monopoly capital was still producing money for those who had the guts to stick it out, despite the complete and utter failure of government projects.

However, there was a massive loss of human capital! Relocation agencies were popping up like mushrooms in every city, with encouraging slogans like, 'The American Dream', and 'Start again in the UK!', 'A new life awaits you in Australia!' Many families applied to these agencies, and in a nutshell, it was a ticket out of South Africa to a new home and a new life, a new start free from corruption and the state's failure to provide a safer life.

All that the new countries of destination required, was that you brought your talents and your brainpower, and in most cases, a little cash would help! Mainly, a solid work ethic and a desire to give your best were all that was needed. It is a known fact that South Africans are hard workers, and so the 'brain drain' started! This removal of intellectual capital would prove to be the very worst product of reverse apartheid!

The cream of South African entrepreneurs, businessmen and women, professionals and progressive thinkers, would be taken out of the South African economy slowly but surely over the next few years. David's son, Sean, and his family were one such family that packed their bags, and a container of their household goods, and left for a new and better life overseas.

Sean and his wife, both had multiple university degrees but were tired of the fact that because of their skin colour, there was no longer a place for them in the South African economy. They had also had enough of the constant stream of bad news about the goings on in the country.

David's family were not the only ones affected. Hundreds of thousands of disillusioned White families just 'upped sticks' and left the country, taking with them thousands of combined years of experience. New lands welcomed this brain bonanza with open arms. Time would show that in the streets of Dallas, Texas, and Perth, Australia, Afrikaans could be heard as South Africans emigrated. Churches were built in Australia to accommodate the ballooning ex-pats from South Africa.

"Good riddance," said the majority of the population left behind. "We don't need them. We can fill their places with our own cadres and political appointees!" But the masses would prove to be wrong in their misguided thoughts! Time would teach that no economy could survive the transfer of years of experience and expertise to another country!

And so, the great failures, forming giant cracks in the economy, quickly started to show! First to fail were rural municipalities, ones that had survived for multiple decades prior to the present time. They were never rich but had collected the rates each month, had provided good civic services, and with the money they received, each municipality was able to pay their staff and their bills.

But, the new 'money for chommies' was soon the order of the day, and the mayors of these small district municipalities were political appointees, who had little or no knowledge of the day-to-day running of a town. The next appointees were city managers, who also had no knowledge or experience, of what was expected. Finally, the so-called elected councillors enjoyed the prominence of their positions, but through no fault of their own, they lacked the necessary skills and expertise to run their portfolios. However, Mercedes Benz and 4x4s became the status symbol of these positions; municipal budgets were disregarded, and councils collapsed financially, one after the other.

Eskom, the power supply authority, supplied power to these councils, the councils supplied electricity to the residents of their areas and collected their payments, but they neglected to pay Eskom for the power supplied in the first place! The result was town councils did not balance the most simple of budgets, and Eskom rapidly started to feel the pinch.

Would the government intervene? The answer was no! Their complete voting base was in these rural areas, and no one was prepared to admit that they had made the mistake of getting rid of the expertise that had run these town councils efficiently for years!

The bigger picture, that of the major cities and metropolises, was the same as the smaller councils, but on a larger scale. This included astronomically high salaries, perks that included upmarket vehicles, and in many cases, unnecessary and unwarranted bodyguards driving cars with blue lights. If it wasn't true, it would be laughable. Meanwhile, the poor became poorer, and the intensity of the brain drain escalated with each passing day.

In the Porter-Smith household, as was the case with many other middle-income families, children and grandchildren left the country for foreign shores, never to return, and so parents and grandparents were left at home by themselves.

This lack of a younger generation was felt in sports clubs and churches. Did the ruling party government care? No! It was reverse apartheid, and the perpetrators of the original apartheid must pay the price!

Chapter 31

Conclusion

South Africans, both Black and White and all those in between swallowed the proverbial pill that fuelled the start of this narrative.

This bitter pill has brought hardship and misery and has done little to administer to the wounds and heartache it has caused.

Through the eyes, and situations, of three different families, we have seen how evil politics will spoil, and even kill, the aspirations of ordinary people – people who could easily be our next-door neighbours, or the family who pulls up next to us in traffic.

Who is right? Who is wrong? Who should have sympathy? Who should forgive? Who should forget? This is anybody's guess! The point is, we have all lost. There are no winners in this game.

Is there any value in speculation? What is in the future, as this pill runs its final course?

Is there anything that the Porter-Smiths, the Khumalos and the Van Wyks can do? The answer has got to be, 'Yes!' We need to believe in a better life for us all. We need to believe that there is dignity in life, and we need to work towards a common goal. Pettiness, suspicion, and hate need to be eradicated and become a thing of the past!

Let us take the very best of each of our cultures, and hone a culture that can be called 'Brand South Africa'. Let us take what we have so graciously been given, and build it up so that we can hand our children the brightest star that the world has ever experienced.

Is it possible? Of course! The pill has run its course. Both half-lives have now been spent!